Longbourn Library
A Novel of Pride, Prejudice, and Books

Trudy Wallis

For Tiffany—sister and Janeite

Chapter 1

A single man of good intellect must be in want of a library card.

Or, so I thought when I became a librarian here at Longbourn Library in Hertford, Idaho. I believed the most intelligent men in the city would be drawn to this hub of reading. In my imagination, these men would stride in, hair disheveled like Einstein, their minds primed for conversations about Sartre and Camus. Instead, I find myself talking to men who *need* to read. *Desperately.*

"You have a dollar fifty late fee," I tell the greasy man in front of me.

"No way. Which books were late?"

I check the computer. "That would be *Secrets to Six Pack Abs, Hair Loss Prevention*, and *Dating for Dummies*."

"Nope. I never checked those out."

"They are tied to *your* library card number."

"That musta been my brother. He does that. Seriously, *why* would I need any of those books?"

He gives me a cocky smile and leans on the counter. His comb-over is obvious.

It has been a long day. "Fine, sir. I'll delete the fees. Don't let your brother borrow your card. He can get his own."

"Right on."

I make a few clicks on the computer and whip out the scanner. I scan in his latest batch of books: *More Secrets to Six Pack Abs, Hair Loss Solutions*, and *Dating Tips for the Unemployed*.

I glare at him as he struts out, his farmer-tanned arm wrapped around the books. My nails dig into the chair's armrests. I take a deep breath and start to wave over the next winner.

"I'll take over for a while, Liz." Jane's voice is gentle. I can always count on Jane.

"Thank you. Really. Thank you, dear."

Jane is reliably sweet in the face of stupidity, but I struggle. For a former beauty queen (Miss Hertford), Jane is remarkably down-to-earth. She and I manage the checkout desk and other odds and ends. Her sweetness and comeliness keep the male patrons coming in.

There are five librarians here on the first floor of Longbourn, including Jane and me.

Mary is the bespectacled girl with no idea of what makeup or tweezers are. She lords over the reference desk. Mary is often bored, as our more established patrons will avoid her desk. That is not to say Mary is not knowledgeable—it is just that her expertise borders on the obscure. Her realm of knowledge seems to be stuck in theology and early 19th century British literature. If a patron dares ask her a question, they often come away from her desk more confused than before.

The bouncy-haired blonde Kathryn (Kitty) keeps up the children's section, which we refer to as "Kitty's Korner." For one fresh out of college, Kitty is competent at her job organizing and maintaining her section, directing parents and children to books she is sure they will enjoy. The children love to call her Miss Kitty and laugh at her name.

Kitty's youth means she is heavily influenced by the even younger and more frivolous Lydia. Lydia is the girl in tight jeans and heavy lip gloss. Lydia's primary job is to shelve books for Longbourn. It is a job she is easily distracted from, especially by the good-looking (or not so good-looking) male patrons. She is only here biding her time, waiting for an inheritance she will get on her 21st birthday.

"Longbourn Library: dedicated to the improvement of one's mind by extensive reading." That is what the sign at the entrance says, anyway.

On the second floor, I hang the last of the notices. The notice reads: "In light of recent events, no potato chips will be allowed in the library."

I grab the box of pushpins and head down the stairs.

"Did you see those fine gentlemen that came in earlier?" It is Mrs. Bennet. She is the retired woman who lives in the house across the street. Her husband comes to read uninterrupted in the striped chair. She comes to gossip.

I humor her. "Can't say that I did." I sit down under the sign that says "checkout." Jane, who has been handling the slow time alone, smiles at me.

Kitty and Lydia come over to listen.

Mrs. Bennet pulls up a chair. She loves an audience. "They are both incredibly handsome and *single*."

Mrs. Bennet hesitates as though waiting for our reaction. Then the verbal diarrhea kicks in. "Charlie—that's what his friend called him—is tall, blond, nicely-dressed. California accent, I am sure. I followed them around the place, but *very* discreetly. You know, I pretended to need a book off the shelf next to them and other clever moves. I heard them discussing books—well, one book in particular called *Pemberley*. This piqued my interest because my husband grunted the other day and put that book down and said it was a satisfying read.

Then he promptly fell asleep, poor fellow. *Anyhow*, Charlie and his friend, I think his name is Darby or something, were here a good half hour just picking up books because, as you know, this is the place to get them. That Darby fellow was wearing a suit and didn't crack a smile the whole time—he kept saying how "inadequate" this library is—but he seemed an intelligent person, since in the end his friend Charlie checked out five books and he checked out *ten*."

"Ten books? The maximum? Well, surely that makes him handsome," I joke.

Jane laughs. "His name is *Darcy*."

"Yes, that's it," confirms Mrs. Bennet. "The handsome, dark-haired Darcy. *Single* Darcy."

"This is the latest addition to Longbourn."

I see Kate de Bourgh's red lipstick moving, but I do not know what she is referring to. She taps her left Gucci shoe and rolls her eyes.

"Oh, for heaven's sake, girl. Get that painting out!" Even when Kate yells, her words are carefully enunciated.

Her assistant, a frazzled young woman, begins to tug at the brown paper on the painting's frame.

Kate de Bourgh is the city official that manages funding for Longbourn Library. She likes to approve outlandish details for the library such as antique lace curtains and elaborate woodwork. She forgets this is not an estate. It is a *library*. After all the "embellishments" are purchased, there is little money left for important things like books.

"This will help Hertford get a bit of culture when they come to the library," Kate declares. Kate's arm makes a grand flourish in the air.

Finally, the painting is unveiled.

At first, I am not sure what I am looking at. It is nothing but gobs of blue, red, brown, and pink oil paint. The painting is a hideous mess—a child's finger painting a parent would hang on a refrigerator for all of a day.

Kate waits.

I cannot think of an appropriate response. "Ahh. *Culture*. Thank you for that," I finally say.

"See that it is hung in a prominent place where the patrons can ponder it best," Kate says.

I know there will be more mocking than pondering, but I am ready to do my job.

Kate leaves a cloud of Chanel no. 5 in her wake as she exits the library.

I hang the painting in a less "prominent" place, on the opposite wall and in the corner. I walk around the area until I am satisfied it is nearly hidden from the general public. *Done.*

Coming back to the checkout desk, I see a striking blond man talking to Jane. Her face is particularly attentive and pleasant as she talks to him. The glimmer in her eyes tells me she is enjoying herself.

I slide behind the desk to take a better look at the man's tanned face. He is completely entranced by Jane's words. She tells him, "If you're going for adventure, try *The Count of Monte Cristo*. It has mystery, subterfuge, a prison break, sword fighting, lost treasure. . ."

"Any romance?"

"Yes. That too." She holds his gaze.

"Okay. I will get that one now. Just a moment." He is like a large child, giddy and bright.

"It's under 'Dumas,'" I tell him so he does not have to search the whole library. "D-U-M-A-S." He scans the rows of fiction with his finger in the air. He comes to the D's and starts toward them. His happy dash stops at the sound of a curt voice.

"We don't have time. Let's go, Charlie."

Who the. . .? I turn in my chair.

A tall man in a black suit is holding a stack of books with a checkout slip sitting on top. Dark hair, sideburns. Handsome—certainly regal in a Laurence-Olivier kind of way. And, based on the sneer on his face, a total killjoy. Must be that "Darcy."

He says to Charlie, "*Monte Cristo* is a classic. I'm sure no one in this town will check it out before our next trip."

Rude.

Charlie comes back like an obedient puppy. "Okay. Next time, for sure. Thank you, Jane. And, umm. . ." He genuinely looks as though he is trying to remember my name, though I have never met him.

"It's Liz."

"*Liz.* Short for Elizabeth, I presume." He holds out his hand. "I'm Charlie."

I am pleased to take his hand. "*Charlie.* Short for Charles?"

"Yes. Well, *no*, now that I think about it." He goes to hand Jane the stack of books, but the conundrum pauses the action mid-air. "It's the same number of letters, actually, but 'Charlie' has that extra syllable. . ."

"We're late, Charlie," his friend gripes. "We'll really have trouble if we have to wait for cows to cross the road again."

As Jane scans in Charlie's books, I look directly at Darcy, and it takes him a few seconds to realize it. He is instantly uncomfortable.

"I'm Liz," I say.

He clutches his books tightly. "Darcy. Well, I'm Will."

"You *will* what?"

"No, ummm. . . Will for William. William Darcy."

So, that is the suit's name. "Mr. Darcy, you're welcome to our little library."

"Thank you." He looks about the room. I have a feeling that he wants nothing more than for this moment to end.

Finally, Charlie gives us a polite goodbye. Darcy simply turns on his heels. I watch his polished shoes travel as he removes himself from the "inadequate" Longbourn Library.

Californians. What can you do? They hear of quiet, conservative Idaho, full of mountains, potato fields, and small cities with growth potential, then pack their vacation bags. Some even sell their tiny homes in Southern Cali and buy a stately Idaho home on six acres, leaving themselves plenty of moolah to spare.

"They are taking over the state," is the general consensus. "These Californians don't move here for a change from their way of life. They want to change *our* state into *theirs*." It is always said with disdain, often with a spit of tobacco for emphasis. Most true Idahoans consider the stunning nature and easy-going atmosphere of our state to be a carefully-guarded secret—one that never should have gotten out.

A few native Idahoans have welcomed the outsiders and their money, but most have felt imposed on. The Hummers drive up and the torches and pitchforks come out. Blogs with titles such as "I Hate Californians" pop up on the Internet and soon have thousands of Idahoan followers. It is as if the whole state collectively rolled up the welcome mat and started swatting the intruders away.

It is them versus us. And Will Darcy appears to be the epitome of "them."

Get thee hence, Darcy.

I like that Charlie guy, at least. I look to Jane, who is smiling to herself. "Well done, Jane," I say. "Very well done."

She nods, then bashfully goes to the D's for a copy of *Monte Cristo* to put on hold for Charles Bingley.

Chapter 2

"Give me something to do. I can't just stand here," Charlotte says as she enters The Hemingway Room, our largest gathering room. Charlotte, a good friend of mine, is 34 and lives with her father in the middle of town. She shows up every week for the library's Tuesday Tea. Instantly, she is in helpful mode—putting forks out and placing napkins "just so" on the tables. I put the lavender tea leaves into the pot to steep.

Charlotte always thought she would have children, stacks of them. She dreamed of being that busy, useful person she is trying to be now. But, she is plain in an era that emphasizes beauty. She is practical in an age that values drama. I have tried setting her up, but the men do not call back. With her mousy hair and bland features, she is not the trophy most men are looking for.

"Are these your doilies, Charlotte?" Lydia teases, taking one off the table and twirling it in the air.

"They are the ones I made, if that is what you mean. They belong to the library."

"How exciting to crochet. You will have to teach me sometime." And Lydia is off like a whirlwind.

"How's your love life, Charlotte?" I ask.

She sighs. "You are the only one who asks anymore, Liz. How telling is that? They've all given up on me." She places the last of the napkins.

"I haven't. I won't."

"How's yours?"

"I was asked out by a guy at the laundromat. He said his name is Junior. He couldn't remember the last book he's read."

"Not for you."

"*No*," I laugh. "You know I've always wanted to spend my life with a reader. Two people under the same roof, enjoying the same books—that's my idea of heaven."

Charlotte, sensible as ever, responds, "I don't think you can be too picky, Liz. I was picky for years and look where it got me."

"You didn't settle. That speaks to your strength."

"No. It speaks to my pride. There's no room for that now."

"That is not sound thinking, Charlotte." I hug my friend. I hate to hear her talk like that.

We have about a dozen people from the community show up for our Tuesday Tea. I make the rounds, welcoming each one. Mrs. Bennet and her best friend, the prim Mrs. Phillips, create a voluble pair in the corner.

Jane is today's reader. She chose to read "Love's Philosophy" by Percy Bysshe Shelley. She begins:

> *The fountains mingle with the river*
> *And the rivers with the ocean,*
> *The winds of heaven mix for ever*
> *With a sweet emotion;*
> *Nothing in the world is single;*
> *All things by a law divine*
> *In one spirit meet and mingle.*
> *Why not I with thine?—*

I just melt into the words. I have to sit down. The patrons in the room are equally mesmerized by the poetry and the way Jane's lovely voice enhances its meaning. I imagine we are all sitting on a mountain and the words of the poem emerge from a tranquil stream. How swiftly a few words can set a soul at rest.

> *See the mountains kiss high heaven*
> *And the waves clasp one another;*
> *No sister-flower would be forgiven*
> *If it disdained its brother;*
> *And the sunlight clasps the earth*
> *And the moonbeams kiss the sea:*
> *What is all this sweet work worth*
> *If thou kiss not me?*

It is hard to snap out of that dream. Once the reading is over, Kitty puts on some light, melodic music to add to the mood. Jane directs a few patrons to the library's poetry section where they latch onto some Shelley poetry collections to check out.

The Tuesday Tea chatter reminds me of the best things in life: treats, books, and the people who love them.

Charlie is thrilled that Jane kept a copy of *Monte Cristo* for him. "That was so kind of you," he says over and over to Jane. "I will be sure to read it, first page to last. Then we will discuss it at length, I'm sure." He immediately cracks open the book, then sits down at a nearby table to make sense of the words inside.

Darcy clearly does not harbor his friend's enthusiasm. He rolls his eyes and unloads his ten books into the return box.

I turn my back to him and imitate his roll of the eyes. Jane starts to laugh, then politely suppresses the laugh into a cough.

Mrs. Bennet blocks Darcy's way as he tries to get to the closest computer.

"Ma'am," he says and half bows toward her.

Mrs. Bennet twirls a ring of her gray hair, then gets to the point. "I understand you do not come here to Hertford often."

Darcy's face shows a twitch of alarm. He surely had no idea his life was fodder for discussion amongst the locals.

"That is correct," he says and tries to move past her.

"And what do think of our little city?" Her face is lit up, anticipating a positive response.

Darcy steps around her and starts to back away. "I would say it is tolerable."

Mrs. Bennet's eyebrows lift. That was not the answer she is looking for. "*Tolerable*? I will have you know, we are home to *the largest* potato farm in Idaho. It's just outside of Hertford. And we have *twenty-five more* that are all nearly as impressive." She gives Darcy a "so *there*" look.

His face is stone cold. "Sounds riveting. Excuse me, ma'am." He swiftly heads for our second computer on the opposite side of the room.

Mrs. Bennet walks deliberately, slowly past the checkout desk. She makes a show of checking that Darcy is no longer in hearing distance, though we all know she would not care if he were.

"The *nerve* of that man," Mrs. Bennet says in semi-whispery voice that draws more attention than it deters. She is rather smug as she saunters toward her husband who is deeply engrossed in *The Quiet Man*. Mr. Bennet's grunt at her approach causes her to casually change course toward Mrs. Young's office, as though she meant to go there all along.

Even Jane cannot stop herself from giggling. However, her polite nature takes over and she collects herself at the sight of a family of patrons coming toward the desk.

Unlike Jane, I do not even attempt to subdue my laughter. As I find I cannot contain a particularly loud burst of chuckling, I see Darcy's head turn toward me. Maybe it is the sideburns and how they move with his profile, but another onslaught of silliness hits me. More laughter ensues and tears fill my eyes.

As my father would say, "What do we live for, but to make our neighbors laugh and laugh at them in our turn?" No harm in laughing at a Californian snob and the gossipy old biddy that tries to show him up.

Charlie looks up from *Monte Cristo* with no sign of understanding what is going on. He smiles at Jane; she blushes back.

I head to Albertson's supermarket after work. I need cat food for Mrs. Hill (my cat). She is very particular about the brand and type. I am never quite sure what she will be in the mood for. I stare at the cat treat shelves a while then choose several kinds. I pray I can read her mind when the time comes.

I stop at the rack of free publications on the way out. A real estate guide catches my eye. The house on the cover is the ultimate dream home. Three stories; swimming pool. The sale tag screams that it was *Reduced by $20,000!* Wow. As soon as the library quadruples my salary and I save for ten years, I can handle a down payment. I flip to the cheaper houses, the ones I could find in the old town neighborhood. Even then, I am a long way off. I squirrel away what money I can, but I imagine I will be living in my one-bedroom apartment for a long time.

"Are you looking to buy a house?" I hear a male voice say.

I glance up.

Whoa. Hottie alert. I nearly forget the question as I take in the whole picture: broad shoulders, dress shirt, and soft, expressive eyes.

"Umm, *no*. It's not feasible right now," I fumble. "Just. . .just dreaming."

"Nothing wrong with that."

I get so caught up memorizing his face, I forget I should continue the conversation. "I suppose you're an agent?" I ask, forcing my words out.

"A secret agent? No. I couldn't tell you that." He has dimples when he smiles. Really nice dimples.

"No. The *other* kind. A secret agent masquerading as a real estate agent."

"You got it. I'd love to show you around some properties sometime. The kind for every budget."

"Well, do you have a card?"

He feels his pockets. "Ah. I must have left my cards at home. Do you have a pen?"

"Always." I pull one out of my purse.

He grins. "If you could have any house in this magazine, which one would it be?"

"The one on the cover."

"Excellent choice. You have an eye for beauty." He scribbles on the cover.

When he is done, I see he has written "Dare to dream!" Then beside it, a phone number and the name *John Wickham*.

"You know my name. May I know yours?" he asks. His face is a whole story. It is enthusiasm and sincerity and regard. I just cannot get over the dimples.

I suddenly remember myself, "It's Liz. Yes, that's it."

"Pleasure to meet you, Liz." John's gaze is direct and confident. He holds out his hand.

"You too, John." As he steps forward to shake my hand, I catch a whiff of his cologne and my senses go mad, causing me to squeeze his hand tighter.

I walk away a bit dizzy, the magazine tucked under my arm and a fist around the bags of cat treats.

I am a different person the rest of the day. I am in a state of bliss. I hum my way through the drive home. I sing love songs as I put away the groceries. I recite exotic Nizar Qabbani poems as I shake cat food into the dish.

However, Mrs. Hill does not notice anything except that I gave her the chicken treats when she wanted the tuna.

My father has a good laugh over my story of a little patron crying because she saw another child checking out "her" book. He loves kids. I wish he had more than just me.

Our phone conversations every Sunday and Wednesday are our main connection as his diabetes confines him to a long-term care facility for veterans in Boise.

"Have you met anyone?" he asks.

There it is. That inevitable question.

"I meet people all day long. It's kind of my job, Dad."

"You know what I mean. The single male kind."

"Yeah, I figured. I've met several of those. One's stuck on Jane. One's a *total* snob. The other is a charming *maybe*."

"So, it *might* be something, at least."

"The cautious side of me says so. It's all wait-and-see."

"I'd love to hold a grandkid before my arms stop working entirely."

"No pressure or anything?"

"Not at all. I could be dead by morning."

"That's not enough time to gestate a grandchild, so I guess you're out of luck."

He laughs like a donkey and that makes me laugh too. What a marvelous grandfather he would make.

"Love you, Lizzie."

"Love you back." I feel the universe coming back into focus. My father always does that for me. He is my soundboard, my touchstone, my family.

I am lost in *Pemberley*.

I read it on break times and stolen moments all day. It is the story of a family struggling to hold onto their entailed estate. The story combines the fierceness of *Gone with the Wind*, the wit of *Emma*, and the subtlety of *The Age of Innocence*. The characters are sharp, real in their humanness, and honest in emotion. Within the pages of *Pemberley*, the heartbreak of unrequited love crackles in the dialogue. Questions of loyalty, both to family and to country are answered without ever being asked.

I find myself particularly attached to the character of Thomas Wiley. Tragedy after tragedy befalls him, but he continues on, clinging to Pemberley as though the world will end if he does not. I imagine him as this sinewy, complicated man in a British cutaway coat. He is honor-bound and courteous. A *true* gentleman.

I sigh every time he shows up on page. Before I even finish the book, I add Thomas to my long list of fictional heroes I am in love with.

I feel as though I am wandering the halls of Pemberley estate, searching for my own soul. *Pemberley* is exactly my kind of book.

Chapter 3

It is 10:00 on a Saturday morning, so an antsy group of children and parents are gathered in Kitty's Korner, waiting to watch the latest puppet show. Denny from the 2nd floor is hiding behind the puppet stage with the Louis Hamm puppet on his fist.

"Has anyone seen Lady Ambrosia?" Kitty asks her audience.

Eyes start darting around the room. Kitty throws her voice, "I'm over here, Miss Kitty." It is a British, pretentious voice. Kitty faces the audience again. "Did you hear that? She must be around here somewhere."

A four-year-old girl shouts, "But *where* is she?"

Kitty takes a step back.

Lady Ambrosia says, "You're getting warmer, Miss Kitty."

Kitty speculates, "I think she might be behind that stage." The kids start standing up to get a better look. Kitty slides behind the stage.

Lady Ambrosia pops up inside the stage window. "I'm right here, boys and girls!"

Lady Ambrosia is a pig princess, kind of a Miss-Piggy-meets-the-Mona-Lisa. The kids clap at the sight of her.

Today's puppet show is a classic story of mistaken identity. Lady Ambrosia encounters another pig whom she believes is a peasant (Louis Hamm). After a great deal of drama, he declares his love, but the Lady herself is torn between her sense of nobility and her little pig heart.

"Oh, Louis Hamm (snort!), I *do* love you!" she finally decides.

"I am not Louis Hamm," the pig face says. "I'm *Prince*

Porkchop."

The kids *ooh* and *aah*.

"The pig girl's stupid," one ten-year-old girl tells her mother at the back of the audience. "*Such* a snob."

"I agree she is prideful," says her mother. "Do you think pride is a good thing or a bad thing?"

As the girl thinks, Mary comes straight over, prepared to deliver a sermon on the subject. Mary clears her throat, then begins, "By all that I have read, I am convinced that pride is very common; human nature is particularly prone to it, and that there are very few of us who do not have it..."

Then follows the mind-numbing discourse. The mother tries to thank Mary and excuse her daughter, but Mary is determined to make an impression. Mary uses words such as "self-glorification" and other large, abstract words that cause the girl's eyes to gloss over.

A little boy comes closer and stares at Mary as she carries on. Sadly, he is far more interested in the giant pimple on Mary's nose than any philosophy coming from her mouth.

I will hand it to Mary: she has no maternal instinct and knows precisely how to bore children to tears. Following her mini-lecture, Mary says, "There is nothing more advantageous to young women as this instruction."

Mary hands the astonished mother a copy of *Fordyce's Sermons*, a book on "all things moral" written 200 years ago for young women by a man who had probably never talked to a woman in his life. And, *that* is why Longbourn Library patrons avoid the reference desk.

Recently, Kate de Bourgh's luck has turned. There are rumors her latest assistant is suitably obsequious and they get along quite well. She brings him into the library, leads him around the room, introduces him as her trusted assistant. I take one look at his profile from afar—the face donning round glasses—and I lose my grip on the books I am holding. The books hit my toes.

Without a doubt, that face belongs to *Collin*.

I gather up the books from the floor. My fingers suddenly cannot move properly. I flop the books up onto the desk one-by-one as flashes of my history with Collin zip through my mind.

I had a horrible blind date with Collin six months ago. A really, *really* bad date. He fed me slimy, over-rehearsed pickup lines the whole evening. He tried to get me to dance to music no sane person could dance to. He told me stories of his childhood that were supposed to be amusing, but were decidedly disturbing. I have never met anyone who was so little self-aware. When he said, "It's clear to me you've had a wonderful time," I knew he was both blind and stupid. I quickly lost his number. And my phone. I also stopped talking to the alleged friend who set us up.

"Liz!" Collin shouts and grabs my hand to shake it. "I thought you had moved. Oh, my *goodness*. What an amazing coincidence!"

"You two know each other?" asks Kate.

"We dated," he says with a giggly sigh, finally releasing my hand, "but then the fates intervened."

"Well, they seem to have intervened again," Kate de Bourgh says, but she is hardly interested. She steps away.

Mrs. Bennet watches this scene unfold, trembling with the privy gossip to follow. Jane looks on, as dumbfounded as I. I hear one of Lydia's snickers from behind a shelf.

I pry out the last of my manners. "I'm happy to see Mrs. de

Bourgh has found such a capable assistant."

"You are *most* kind. Did you hurt yourself when you fell from heaven, my angel?"

Oh, good grief, *no*. The hand he released feels sweaty. I feel slimed head to toe.

He explains to all who are listening, "I find these little compliments don't hurt with the ladies." He winks at me.

Kate de Bourgh drops her bag and jacket on the floor and her lackey Collin duly runs to get them. She goes about her business, explaining the pieces of art as he superfluously compliments every ugly one. He takes copious notes and hangs on each utterance.

When Collin comes back to the desk to say farewell, I am nowhere to be found.

Mr. Bennet was correct. *Pemberley* is a satisfying read. I put it down, but it is still there around me. I completely absorbed the world described in the book. Upon reading the final page, I find myself mourning the character of Thomas as though he has died.

How does one have a funeral for a fictional character? I start writing the eulogy in my head: "Today we say goodbye to Thomas Wiley—hero, nobleman, and hottie with a naughty body. . ."

I live the rest of the day inside the walls of Pemberley. I surely need some advanced alien surgery to remove the dream and reconnect to the real world. What did Sherwood Anderson say? "I cannot shake myself out of myself." I cannot do it either, and then wonder why anyone would want to.

"I'm next," says Mary, and takes the book away from me.

Most of the librarians have read *Pemberley* now. The author,

William Fitz, will do a public reading next week in Hertford and these things are made more special if one reads the book first. I can see why Jane so earnestly recommended it to me and several patrons.

Jane also insisted Charlie read it. Surprisingly, he claimed he already had.

"A Blind Date with a Book" reads the sign. It is one of the creative ways we try to get patrons interested in books, as well as make some money for the library. We librarians spent all our extra time the last two days wrapping thick paper around "retired" books and writing a simple blurb about what type of book was inside. For a whopping $2, a patron can take home their surprise book.

We presorted the books by genre, so we would each take a pile and not waste time overthinking our blurbs. Kitty took the romance pile, Jane the classics, and I the mysteries. Lydia grabbed the Westerns, saying something about having "a thing" for cowboys. Finally, we put up a display and soon people began to take their blind date books home.

It seemed simple enough.

Soon I noticed Lydia taking particular pains telling the good-looking male patrons about the opportunity to buy a book. She guided them to the display, then, no matter what kind of books they claimed to like, she pushed them toward the Westerns.

It was a busy day with no time to stop and suspect something underhanded in Lydia's movements. Just Lydia being Lydia. Flirting as usual.

At the end of the day, I am left to lock up. As I turn the key, I startle at the sight of a man standing just outside the door. He is leaning against the building as though posing for a Marlboro ad. He looks me up and down.

"Are you. . .*Lydia*?" he asks, the flirtation obvious. He is holding a paperback Western along with its ripped paper wrapping.

"I'm not." My hand starts searching my pocket for my can of Mace. *Where is it?*

"That's too bad. I was hoping we could schedule that date. I don't suppose *all* the librarians are up for it?"

Alarm bells go off in my head. "Huh?"

He whips open the cover of *The Shootist* and reads: "How about a real date with a real woman? Lydia, *two-three-five. . .*"

Oh, bloody Lydia. I snatch the book from him.

"Hey!"

"It's against library policy for librarians to give out their phone numbers. I will gladly refund your money." I am hoping he cannot remember the number.

"So. . .no number. Just a date?"

"No date!"

I hand him two bucks and send him on his way.

I stomp back into the library. After taking a moment to shake off the "ick," I drop *The Shootist* onto the counter. I gather all the Westerns from the date-with-a-book display. With a surge of angry resolution, I start to rip the wrapping off all the Westerns and swipe a permanent marker over the number for Lydia's "escort service."

A few minutes ago, all I wanted was to go home at the end of a long day. I am furious at this latest example of Lydia's nonsense. What is worse, I know *nothing* will change, no matter how many warnings she gets. Her status as goddaughter to Mrs. Young, the head librarian, practically ensures her immunity.

"Besides, Lydia will be leaving us soon," is what Mrs. Young will say. I am helpless in the face of this logic. Ugh.

Rip, rip, rip.

The old wrappings get smashed to the bottom of the garbage can. Louis L'Amour, Zane Grey, Dorothy Johnson, Louis Masterson, and Larry McMurtry novels create a haphazard pile.

Book after book emerges into the fluorescent light streaming from above the checkout desk.

Each book is, in a way, a surprise for me as they stir up childhood memories. Some of the Westerns I recall enjoying in a hammock my father had attached to our trailer. Others I remember my father reading as we sat fishing on the Snake River bank.

Under the touch of my fingers, the battered paperbacks whisper their histories. The smells of ink-on-paper rise through the air and cleanse my senses. After several minutes, my fury slows, then subsides.

It turns out there are few things more calming than a quiet room full of books.

In this hushed space, the whoosh of wind against the broad windows is bold. Small sounds are amplified: the crinkle of paper is sharp, the squeak of the marker abrupt and final.

I feel the presence of each book on the shelves with a startling clarity. We have an understanding, the books and I: I am their guardian and they my wards.

As a child, I often dreamed of being locked in the library overnight. I thought for sure, given enough time, I would find a secret passageway tucked behind a rolling bookshelf. I imagined running through the aisles unchecked. If nothing else, I would enjoy reading the forbidden "on hold" books undisturbed until the doors were unlocked at dawn the following morning.

I often forget that dream in the light of day when I am here for work—and much of that work is tedious and less enchanting than I thought it would be. But now the movement of cars past the windows casts a shifting, eerie light on the books.

In my fancy, the library opens to ghostly patrons. Mrs. Louisa Hurst, the sole original librarian of Longbourn Library, floats across the room. I always sensed her noble spirit gliding through Longbourn's shelves, spying on librarians and patrons alike, tucking herself between the pages of books to avoid being seen. Her supernatural route sticks to the original part of the building, ending where the sturdy brick first laid by Hertford settlers meets the wooden seams of the 1950's expansion.

Mrs. Hurst haunts the place she loves best. Not in a freaky-librarian-in-*Ghostbusters* sort of way—more of a woman-longing-for-the-latest-in-paperback type of way. Perhaps it is she who takes over the striped chair every night. Maybe she is there now, dressed in aging lace, thumbing through the pages of *The Shining*.

Wow, what a big shiver. Books will do that.

Okay, done. Same Westerns, new wrapping, new blurbs. All lined up for the picking.

I will be upset with Lydia tomorrow.

As promised, Jane lets me man the desk the next time Charlie and Darcy come in. Mrs. Bennet ascertained through the gossip channel that Darcy is an "aspiring writer." I want to see what an "aspiring writer" does. He does not fail to answer my curiosity.

Darcy takes his time searching the database, referring to scratches of notes he has on a pad. His movements are methodical and calculated as he strides about the rows collecting books. There is not an ounce of frivolity in him and his crisp suit. He is exactly the kind of man I enjoy teasing.

Jane and Charlie are discussing *The Count of Monte Cristo* in the corner. Charlie is animated, Jane subdued, but they both seem to agree on the same points. I marvel that so many years after its publication, *Monte Cristo* is still making such an impact.

In a spare moment, I type Darcy's name into our database. *Nothing*. Not one book by a Will or William Darcy to be found in Longbourn Library.

I suppress some snarky thoughts while he avoids my gaze.

With ten books in hand, Darcy takes a few steps toward the checkout, then looks at me. He seems taken aback by the smile on my face. The smile is guileless—just the result of trying to withhold my natural thoughts.

"I can help you right here," I say cheerfully.

Ten more books. I scrutinize the stack carefully. *The History of Underclothes, The Basics of Corset Building, History Drawers On: The Evolution of Women's Knickers*. . . Most of them have a layer of dust on them.

He clears his throat. "It's research," he states.

I am unimpressed. "Knickers?"

"Well, yes. Miss . . ."

"It's *Ms*."

"*Ms*. Liz. I. . ." He searches the walls of books for words, but I do not let him find any.

"I need your library card," I say.

He looks at his card as though he just realized he has one. "Oh, ummm, *here.*"

I deliberately take a long time scanning each book. I print the checkout sheet and slap it on top of his smutty books. "Due back by the 15th."

"Yes." He takes the stack awkwardly from me.

"Will Darcy," I say wistfully. "Are you coming to Tuesday Tea tomorrow afternoon?"

The suit backs up a step.

"No, *no.*"

"Too wild for you?"

He cannot respond.

"Will *all* of the librarians be there?" asks Charlie, who is now standing behind Darcy.

"Of course."

Charlie grins and looks toward Jane. "Then yes, we will come. And thank you dearly for the invitation."

From the return box, I take the latest batch of children's books. They have cheese powder fingerprints all over them: page after page of little yellow finger-shaped stains. I turn to the final page of *The Boxcar Children*, a personal childhood favorite, and note some yellow powder there next to *The End*. I am satisfied the little patron read the entire book. There is nothing worse than seeing a new book come back without a hint of being read. I delight in those books that have been read so much we have to tape them together. What a glorious thing, this sharing of words, ideas, stories.

Chapter 4

It is Tuesday Tea again. Lydia is preparing to read her poetry selection. The room is unusually full. Mrs. Gardiner, the mayor of Hertford, has shown up and brought a few friends. At least twenty-five people are milling about, holding cups of tea and slices of cheesecake.

I spy Darcy suited up and sitting at the back of the room. Instantly, that familiar itch to tease him courses through me.

"I feel we've gotten off to a bad start, sir," I exclaim as I sit next to him.

He glances toward me and shifts in his chair. "Probably my fault. I don't have the knack for talking to strangers."

"Simply put, you need practice. An assembly such as this is a great opportunity for that." Smile, Darcy. Come on, you arrogant twit.

"Yes. I will confess that much."

"How was the book about knickers, by the way?"

"Fascinating," he says flatly.

"Any other books you'd like to recommend? We do know how to read here in Idaho. Women can vote here, too."

Darcy now turns to look at me, trying to make out the expression on my face. Some people cannot take sarcasm for what it is.

The requests for everyone to sit down interrupt our conversation. I see Charlie sit genially next to Jane. Mrs. Bennet takes immediate notice of this and tells Mrs. Phillips who starts a round of whispers about the matter. The crowd—the usual lovers of refined poetry—settle in. All is calm and splendid for a few moments.

Then all hell breaks loose.

Lydia, loving the spotlight and perhaps wired on tea, begins to read—not an elegant, pithy poem of love, but—a bawdy poem called "Tale of a Brothel." A few lines in and the uncomfortable glances around the room twist my stomach into a queasy mush.

The unease is contagious. Mary, who seems to be wearing a dress from a production of *The Crucible*, stomps out of the room.

Darcy sits up, arms crossed, probably thinking Idahoans would not know what real poetry is if Walt Whitman walked in and wrote *Leaves of Grass* on the wall.

I hope the poem is just a few stanzas long, but the tale weaves on and soon Lydia is flipping the page. Charlotte blushes as Lydia's sing-song voice trills over words like "wanton," "frenzied," and "lecherous."

Mr. Bennet sits on the edge of his chair, an uncharacteristic grin spread across his face. He slaps his knee at the most salacious parts. Mrs. Bennet huffs at him and hits him on the arm.

At least someone is enjoying the debauchery.

Mr. Bennet stands up and claps the loudest when the fiasco concludes. Lydia bows flippantly and laughs at her own joke.

Longbourn Library will be starting a policy pronto that makes sure all poems get approved for Tuesday Tea. I will write the memo myself.

"Tea?" I ask Darcy.

He unfolds his arms. "Yes," he says, then quickly moves toward the refreshment table.

I head toward Charlotte, who just separated herself from Mrs. Bennet.

"So," Charlotte says, then gestures towards Mrs. Bennet, "I hear the love of your life just reconnected with you."

I laugh. She knows the story of Collin and our disaster of a date. "Sure did. It was 'fate.'"

Mary, who is in charge of the music for the event, reenters the room. She sets up the CD player and pushes "play." This wonderful 19th century piano music moves through the whole library.

Charlotte and I sip hot tea and enjoy a polite discussion that steers sublimely clear of brothels. Fresh mint tingles my throat and refreshes my senses.

Charlie separates himself from Jane just long enough to tell me what a lovely time he is having. Darcy remains stiff and unconvinced nearby.

Lydia and Kitty move about the place, sharing gossip and jokes at everyone else's expense. As they ramble past, Lydia snickers and asks, "Where's your boyfriend, Liz?"

I roll my eyes. Lydia and Kitty roar with laughter and wander off to their next victim.

Charlotte quietly observes, "I worry about Jane and this Charlie guy. Look at them. He is all enthusiasm and she is all sweet reserve. She is not trying hard enough. Jane should make the most of every moment she has his attention."

"She is still learning about him and sorting out her feelings."

"When she has a ring on her finger, there will be time for falling in love as much as she wants. She needs to act fast, before he gets away."

"I highly doubt Charlie is going anywhere."

Charlotte whispers, "As for you, there's a tall, handsome man looking at you, Liz."

I scan the room. I can only see Charlie and Darcy. What man?

"In the suit," Charlotte clarifies.

Hmm. "I'm sure it doesn't mean anything. That's Will Darcy from Sacramento. He's very disapproving of us country folks. If he glanced this way, it was only to focus on my flaws."

Just then the next song comes on. Mary stands up and pauses the music. She declares, "I could not find the complete aria with vocals, so I will attempt to sing the vocals myself."

Mary restarts the music and the most ungodly sound emerges from her throat. Her voice is unnervingly off-key and ill-timed. Her guttural consonants overshadow her terrible pronunciation of all words French. Then, as if she needs to offend the ears of every person in the room, she ends the first verse with a bizarre little squeak.

Mr. Bennet, summoning Dorothy Parker, exclaims, "What fresh hell is this?!" Then he jumps up and heads out the door, probably trudging home where there is no shrieking to interfere with his usual quiet reverie.

Mrs. Bennet sighs and says something about her nerves and how easily they get agitated these days.

The whole room is full of people who suddenly either want to leave, or quickly down some cheesecake and leave. *Leave* is the optimum word.

Charlotte is alarmed at the sight of the crowd heading for the door and tries to hold the patrons in place with an offer of lemon bars.

Charlie and Jane continue to chat happily, though Jane lifts a concerned eyebrow with every major squeal Mary belts out. Charlie clearly sees no one and nothing but Jane.

Mary at last finishes her song and an uncomfortable lack of applause forces us all to clap. The applause is graceless, delayed, and horribly, unnecessarily loud. Mary smiles and bows the deep, solemn bow of the proudly humble.

I put a lemon bar on a plate and hand it to Darcy. In a hoity-toity British accent, I ask him, "Would you like some more tea, sir?" I cannot help but do it with a smile.

"I've had enough," he replies dryly.

I am pretty sure the imbecile is not talking about tea.

Mrs. Hill stretches herself across the top of the recliner as I read *A Good Man is Hard to Find.* I am suspended in the grotesque world of Flannery O'Connor, seeing the ordinary in an extraordinary and twisted new way. I must say there is no enjoyment quite like reading.

How long have I been sitting here? One hour? *Three*? The tick of the clock and an occasional hum of purring does little to help me mark the time.

I suddenly stand up. Maybe I should be doing something *social*? It is the weekend, after all. Hertford is not the most happening place, but surely a woman could find a place to go, people to meet?

And perhaps there is a handsome man out there who likes the book-reading-cat-owning type?

Mrs. Bennet's nails-on-chalkboard voice echoes in my head: "Get your nose out of that book, Liz, and find yourself a man!"

Maybe she is correct. I cannot find love by sitting here. It is not as though Juliet met Romeo while reading at home in Verona.

Okay.

I *will* get up.

I *will* get dressed.

I *will* find the love of my life.

Right after I finish this chapter.

I call John Wickham. It is a bit of a pretense, but I did see a little blue house in the real estate magazine I might be able to afford *eventually*. Mostly I would really just like to see John's face again.

"I'd be more than happy to show you around," he readily tells me. I swear I can hear his dimples over the phone.

I park in front of the little blue house. It is resting on a street with a few other properties with "for sale" signs projecting from yellowed front yards. The lawn of the house is unkempt. The windows and steps are filthy. Smoke from the nearby Supreme Spuds potato factory adds a bit of haze to the yard. Despite the scraggly weeds and peeling paint, I have never seen a house so happily situated.

John drives up in a 10-year-old Buick. He strides over. He is wearing a nice striped button-down shirt, dress pants, polished shoes. And he smells like a million bucks.

"What do you think?" he asks with a mega-grin.

It takes me a second to realize he is asking about the house. "It could use some TLC," I say.

"Couldn't we all? Let's take a look at the outside first."

John is relaxed, friendly. He deftly points out the positives in the house: new and sturdy shingles, strong foundation, space for a potential garden. It is a remarkable show of salesmanship.

I ponder the empty house before me. All the spine-tingling ghost stories I read as a child about old, haunted houses make my senses flutter. How strange it would be to say this dusty, creaky place is *my* house. I imagine the ways I could fix it up and make it my own. I think of Mrs. Hill stretched out in the windowsill, warming herself in the one scrap of sunshine she can find. I feel so grown up just anticipating something as normal as buying a house. And, I suddenly wish I were getting Lydia's inheritance so I would not have to pay a mortgage.

I realize, too, I do not want to be alone in the house. I want a good man with me.

"Can we take a look inside?" I ask.

"Absolutely," John insists. He goes to the keypad lock attached to the front door handle. He punches in a few numbers, but the lock does not open.

He says, "Not to worry, not to worry. Just try again."

I love the way nothing seems to faze him. And, I like standing close to him because he smells so darn good, like the woods after a good rain.

John seems to be trying different combinations of numbers, but nothing works. A curious wrinkle develops on his forehead.

"Ah," he surmises, "they don't seem to have the right password installed on this keypad. Maybe they changed it, but didn't let me know. I couldn't say without calling them, but it's lunchtime."

I have no idea who "they" are. "No matter. We can peek through the windows at least?" I suggest.

"Genius. Let's try that."

Through the windows, we can spy the living room, covered in stained flowered wallpaper. The kitchen holds a turquoise refrigerator from the 1960s. The one bedroom we can see is half-hidden by faded green curtains and painted with balloons. I choose a spot on the hardwood floors where I would put my bookshelves. When I have a house of my own, I will be miserable if I do not have an excellent book collection.

The rooms are a bit ragged, but John again turns on his skills and addresses the details that make this house a bargain. I am thoroughly amazed.

There is one high window I cannot quite reach.

"Lift you up?" he brightly offers.

"Too much chocolate these days." I pat my stomach. "I wouldn't want to hurt you."

"I can handle it." He is so self-assured.

He easily lifts me half a foot to peer through the window. The room is dark inside and I can barely see anything. He has strong hands. They feel good around my waist. I forget why I am here for a moment.

"Okay. You can put me down." My feet hit the ground and I find my balance.

"How was that?" he asks. He is only a few inches away and his eyes are looking intently into mine. I feel for a moment I am a heroine in a gothic romance novel and he is the dashing hero set to rescue me.

My hand is still resting on his arm. Reluctantly, I remove it.

"Well, you've given me a lot to think about," I tell him.

"That's the best compliment I've ever received." His smile wins me over.

I am there again: that blissful state. I cannot buy the house. I can barely *hope* to buy the house. I thank him and leave with a sense that good things can come my way, anyhow.

Our big summer event is the Summer Reading Program. It guarantees a steady flow of children, ages five to twelve, coming through our doors. This is our sign-up week, so the paperwork makes a huge impact on our normal workload. We rely heavily on volunteers to explain the program, show children the prizes, and help them set goals. Mrs.

Bennet is one of the volunteers. So is Mr. Bennet, though it is apparent he was hoodwinked into the task. He keeps glaring at the kid reading quietly in "his" striped chair.

"You might want to read more of a variety of books," I tell a freckled boy. He has a list of books to read and they are all of the *Goosebumps* series. I like a good spooky story as much as the next person, but it is good to mix it up a bit. "Miss Kitty over there has some other series, some about superheroes, aliens, true stories, adventure. . ."

"Any that make you. . .*JUMP?!!*" he asks, springing at me. I startle and push my chair back. What a wicked little boy.

He laughs and slaps his list paper against his face.

Ah, the joy of children.

Jane and I are trapped behind the checkout desk all morning. Normally, I would dislike sitting for so long, but helping out the little patrons is diverting at the very least. The thought of John (*sigh!*) keeps me entertained during the dull moments, anyhow.

"You're rather lit up, Liz," Jane notices.

"Am I?"

"What's his name?"

It is hard to say it out loud, as though it is admitting too much. "John. That's a bit of a droll name, but he's just. . . He's got charm. I just need to rob a bank so I can buy a house through him."

"That's all? A girl in love can't do less," she kids.

I go to deny any feelings, but I smile and shrug my shoulders instead.

Jane takes her next stack of books to check in. "Keep me posted on that, all right, Liz?"

As I wave over the next patron, a line of great literary couples travels through my mind: Jane Eyre and Mr. Rochester, Wesley and Buttercup, Anne Elliot and Captain Wentworth.

John and *Liz* Wickham?

I love books. One does not become a librarian without feeling their power first. New books, old books, thin ones, thick ones, banned ones, underrated ones, overrated ones, bestsellers and worstsellers. They are all friends.

The Odd Women grips me. George Gissing's words are seeping in through my skin. I should not be reading on the job, but I cannot seem to help it. I feel as though I *am* the character Rhoda Nunn, champion of women's rights. I am living in England in the late 1800s and the motion of the modern world does little to rattle me. I hear a voice, but it does not register until the words are repeated: "Excuse me, ma'am."

"Yes." I forcibly push the book onto the desk. I must. "Yes?"

Then I am off, helping a woman use the search system on one of the public computers. It is a routine click-and-type-here explanation that leaves the woman confident she can handle the next phase of the search.

On my way back to my seat, I hear Charlie's voice coming from behind a shelf.

He says, "I've noticed you glancing her way time and again. Admit it."

The next voice is Darcy's. "I'm impressed with her fine taste in books. That is all."

Wow. I thought Darcy would never come back here after that last Tuesday Tea tragedy.

I try to figure out whom they could be talking about. I survey the library. Kitty is in her Korner organizing her display of Maurice Sendak books. Mary is patronizing a patron at the reference desk. Mrs. Phillips is surreptitiously adding a lewd novel to her checkout stack of gardening books. Jane is politely listening to the latest "scandal" Mrs. Bennet has to offer. The only woman reading is Lydia, who has stopped to look through a book off the cart. The book's cover says *Everyone Poops*.

Fine taste indeed.

My conversation with my father veers all over tonight. One moment we are talking about the little blue house, the next we are arguing over the existence of Bigfoot. As usual, all topics are open for discussion except the topic of my mother.

My father tells me, "I am half-way through *Pemberley*. You were right about it. An intelligent read."

"Isn't it? At one point in the book, I stopped seeing words and felt like I was actually *there*. That is how well-written it is."

"Did this guy write anything else?"

"Nope. It is his debut novel."

"He has a solid career in front of him."

"I sure hope so."

"Can you handle the wait for his next book?" he asks in his kidding voice.

A wave of impatience and anxiety hits me. "I never know. Waiting for "the next book" is my constant agony. There was nothing worse than waiting for the 7th *Harry Potter*, for example. There was a desperate moment I even begged God to spare J.K. Rowling *and me* until the series was complete."

My father's donkey laughter makes the phone hum. "That's my daughter. So many books, so little time."

Chapter 5

As often happens in summer, Longbourn Library has a sudden infestation of earwigs. Lydia is, of course, terrified of them and nearly every other little critter. The latest earwig has the audacity to poke its head up as Lydia is putting a book away. Her scream flies, and the book does too. Lydia yells, "Get it, Liz! Get it, get it, *GET IT*!!" Her fright passes easily to Kitty whose hysteria matches the same pitch as Lydia's. They dash to the bathroom, far from the bug that is taking a leisurely stroll through the library.

Mr. Bennet, in his striped chair, grumbles something under his breath about silly girls and the nonsense he is being forced to listen to. He shifts and relaxes back into *The Invisible Man*.

I get my lucky bug killer (AKA my shoe) and hobble toward the spot Lydia stood in. It takes a minute of crawling on the floor, but I locate the little bug and *Whap!*

Nothing. It just runs a bit faster. *Whap! Whap! Whap!*

Mrs. Bennet solicits the help of the most handsome male patron she can find. He stomps a few times and misses by a mile.

Stomp! Whap! Stomp! Whap! Stomp!

"Is this a hoedown?" It is Kate de Bourgh, hovering over me in silk and suede.

"My apologies, ma'am," I say as I take a final, fatal swing at the earwig. It is certainly dead now. I thank the unfortunate man who got sucked into the situation and slide my shoe back on.

Kate follows me back to the checkout desk.

"You're a curious one, Liz. Where did you go to school?"

"I'm a Vandal."

Her red lipstick parts into a horrified O. "I'm shocked that you'd admit so openly to something like that. Did they not do a background check on you?"

"I don't *vandalize*. I went to the University of Idaho. The *Vandals*? It's their mascot."

She is not impressed. "My daughter, Anne, of course, went to UCLA. But you've probably never heard of that."

"I *have* actually heard of that."

Mrs. Bennet is pretending to read a magazine off the rack. She is hanging on every word.

"My daughter Anne is *so* accomplished," Kate sniffs. "You rarely come across such a genius." She considers, "I suppose you went to *public* school."

"Nope. Homeschooled."

"*Hmm.* Your mother must have been quite the slave to your education."

"Not at all. She ran off with a truck driver when I was five."

"Oh, *my.*"

"Sunshine and books were the mainstays of my education. I wouldn't change it for anything." I say it with confidence, but I feel every inch the rube she thinks I am.

Kate is too repulsed to continue the conversation. She quickly glides away to more important people.

Harvey de Bourgh, God rest his soul, was bamboozled into marriage and was quick to figure out he would rather die than stay in it. So, he died. He left Kate with a fabulously generous inheritance and a young daughter. Kate thinks everyone is as equally dazzled by her wealth as she is. However, we all know she is just as much a hick as we are and it is her money, not her pretensions to "nobility," that wields community standing.

Lydia and Kitty emerge from the bathroom after getting the "all clear."

An exasperated man comes up to the desk. "I can't find nothing I need in this liberry."

And I get to work helping him find the nothing he needs.

It is raining outside, something fierce, as though the storm came directly from *Wuthering Heights*. Thunder rumbles through the bookshelves, shaking the books into tighter huddles. Lightning, stealthy and illuminating, strikes at the weather vanes on farms skirting Hertford. Incandescent flashes take blinding slides through the room. The thud of water pellets echoes from the thick-paned windows.

The fragrance of rain mixes with the smell of old books. It is heavenly—that combination of threat and safety.

Longbourn Library is empty except for a few patrons waiting out the storm. Mr. Bennet seems particularly at home in his comfy striped chair, regardless of time or rain.

I corner Mr. Lucas to ask if he came here on his horse again.

"Nope. Brought the Chevy this time," he says with a cheeky grin.

That is good, both for the horse and for the flower bed. Last time Mr. Lucas rode here on Goober, half of Longbourn's flowers disappeared.

I hear a male voice drifting over from the fiction section. The voice is full of mirth—absolute joy. Charlie is asking Jane once more to recommend a good book as he has already finished her last recommendation, which he cannot say enough good things about.

Mrs. Bennet leans in toward me. "Wasn't he here yesterday as well, Liz?" she whispers, her voice full of mischief and delight.

"Yes. He definitely was."

She sits down, satisfied with my answer.

I pretend to organize books as Jane pulls another masterwork from the shelf and begins to describe it. Charlie does not take his eyes from her face as she speaks.

Jane's passion for books never ceases to radiate. Though she is not terribly articulate on other subjects, with books she finds the perfect words of persuasion while excluding any spoilers. It is an act of sorcery every time, I swear. Not once have I seen her fail to get a patron to take home a book. Patrons often carry their books, trance-like, up to the checkout counter after getting Jane's descriptive, avid suggestions. Of course, it is a bit easier with patrons who are terribly smitten with her. That is decidedly the case with Charlie. He would take a cactus home if Jane recommended it as toilet paper.

Soon Jane comes back to the desk and checks *The Moonstone* out for Charlie. She carefully slides the book into a plastic zip-up bag to spare it from the raging elements.

Charlie analyzes the bag hugging *The Moonstone* and says, "It must be a precious book."

"It is. I would venture to say every book here falls into that category."

"But, this one is particularly special," he theorizes, "because it came from you."

Jane tips her head to the side and smiles. "Have a pleasant day, Mr. Bingley."

"Likewise, Jane. You have been most helpful, you know, as usual." He leaves, clutching the book as though it is his lifeline.

Mrs. Bennet wastes no time coming over to Jane. "What a fine thing for us to see Charlie again. He came in all that weather, too."

Jane smiles slightly, her cheeks starting to color. She looks down at the card on the counter.

"Oh, no. He forgot his library card," Jane says.

Mrs. Bennet runs to the window and looks out in the rain. "He's still here! Hurry, Jane. You can run it out to him."

"Oh, where did I put my coat?" Jane asks desperately.

"There's no time for coats, my dear! Go, *go!*" Mrs. Bennet insists.

Jane, bewildered, holds the tiny card above her head and pushes open the entrance door. And I head to the window.

It is a priceless scene to behold. Charlie nearly leaps from his car at the sight of her. His smile is wide and he gingerly wraps his fingers around the edge of the card, but she doesn't let go.

He says thank you, thank you, *thank you.*

They hold the card between them for a good ten seconds as the rain pummels them. Those last five seconds they are not even talking, just looking at each other. A crack of lightning overhead brings Jane to her senses. She says goodbye and makes her way back inside.

When Jane returns, soaked clean through, I hand her a paper towel. Her hair is resting in soppy tendrils around her face, no thanks to the wind and rain. She looks like Medusa—a happy Medusa.

She turns to me meaningfully and I go to say, "Well, done Jane," but her eyes cross and her mouth opens in a bizarre maw. Her nose crinkles. And she sneezes.

With Jane out sick today, we Longbourn librarians are left filling in. Charlie comes in, confident, then downcast when he hears Jane is sick.

"Sick?!" he echoes. True worry crosses his face.

"Yes," I say, "but we could gladly make a book recommendation for you."

Mary does not hesitate to pull out an 18th century religious tome she is sure he will ponder at length.

"No, it's okay," says Charlie. He is crestfallen. "I prefer Jane. Well, I prefer her *recommendations*."

Charlie visits the next day, bringing a desperate hopefulness with him. He looks to Jane's chair. Empty. I sorely wish I could hand him Jane's phone number.

On the third day, I take in Charlie's defeated countenance and shrug my shoulders.

He then places a single daisy on the counter where Jane usually sits. He looks about the library with tenderness as though committing it to memory. He nods to me and takes a slow exit out.

The daisy is a delicate, sunny bloom. It captures Jane's spirit perfectly. I put it in a vase and it rests there, patient and optimistic, until Jane returns the next day.

Jane walks in refreshed and recovered when she returns. She looks every bit the beauty queen apart from the touch of red around her nose. A new dress and new hair style tell me this return to the library was much-anticipated.

She is particularly blithe in her work. The daisy, a pleasant companion, sits next to her on the desk. She touches it, ponders it, appreciates it every chance she gets.

And every time the entrance swishes open, Jane turns her head to see who is there.

The entire day goes by with no sign of Charlie. He does not show up the next day, either. The following day, a Sunday and day off work, leaves Jane in a state of tortuous concern.

On the day after that, Darcy shows up alone.

Chapter 6

Darcy is going about his usual routine. He enters his list of books in the database, then locates them precisely where they should be. Jane and I are helping a long line of people check out their books. Jane keeps looking toward Darcy, then at the door, certainly wondering if Charlie is simply lagging behind.

It is not long before it becomes clear where he is.

After his usual long, careful book-selection process, Darcy slides his latest stack of books toward me across the checkout desk. It is a hesitant motion, as though he is not sure he is ready for this moment.

I go over the titles and say, "Hmm. Nothing in here that references underwear. Would you like to go back and look? I'm sure we could find you something."

"No, nothing like that today." He is extra wooden. Suit is too tight, perhaps. He does not look at Jane.

Scan. Scan. Scan.

I ask Darcy, "Where is our good friend Charlie this fine day?"

Darcy is slow to answer. "He's moved on. He took a job in New York."

I swear I can hear Jane's heart breaking.

I reply, "That's really too bad. We enjoy his company."

"Of course. But it is probable Charlie will spend very little time in Hertford in the future. These things happen."

I shove the books toward him. He wraps an arm around them and leaves promptly.

I turn to Jane. She is processing what she just heard, playing with the ends of her flowy dress. She sits next to me the next half hour, pretending to be her usual radiant self as she talks to the patrons.

Once the line clears, I start to check in the large pile in the return box. I pull out *The Moonstone*, which Darcy must have returned on Charlie's behalf.

Jane spies the book and goes a shade paler. Instinctively, she reaches for it and circumspectly takes it in hand.

"We had so much to discuss about this one," she says in a whisper.

That is when the tears slip down her face.

Tuesday Tea. The number of attendees has greatly diminished since Lydia and Mary's debacle. Charlotte is here, as usual. She is arranging her homemade petit fours and canapé on a tray. Mariah from the 2nd floor is in charge of today's *tasteful* poetry. Of course Charlie is absent and, in a twist I saw coming, so is Darcy.

I fill up cups of tea to cool.

"I've never seen such an exemplary doily," a slithery voice says.

Oh, no. I know that voice.

I turn around slowly and there is Collin. Powdered sugar from a Danish wedding cookie sticks to his lips. His grin turns his eyes into little slits behind those thick round glasses. "My dear Liz, look at this magnificent setup. Surely this was your brilliant idea," he spits out.

An exit. I look for the nearest exit.

"I can see on your face," says Collin, "you are surprised to see me here. Mrs. Bennet was kind enough to invite me."

"It *was* kind. It was a true act of charity."

"I see you share my opinion. Mrs. Bennet is the most generous and *encouraging* woman."

Topic change. *Now.* "And how do you like your new job, Collin?"

"Splendid. Mrs. de Bourgh is such a classy employer. Her every word shows the superior graces of elevated rank. I've never been better situated. I can't help wondering if *someone* had something to do with me getting the job?" There's a distinct twinkle in his eye.

I nearly throw up. "No. I would *not* have thought of that."

"Then it is, as they say, divine intervention. The stuff of romance novels, perhaps."

It feels like a snake just slithered up my spine. Ugh.

"I have to go to the. . . to the powder room."

"Princess Liz needs to visit her chambers," he says, then bows.

I run toward the restroom. I suppose, like Lydia, I do not like creepy-crawlies, either.

From the corner of my eye, I see Mrs. Bennet scurry over to him, eager no doubt to hear what passed between us.

Lydia is in the restroom, applying extra mascara. She snorts when I come in. "Your boyfriend is here, I see. When's the wedding?"

My face looks weird in the mirror.

I realize that, oddly, I look too done up. *Too* nice. I was never the type to wear flannel and overalls, but lately I have felt I could step it up a bit. Silky shirt, careful makeup. Coifed hair.

It is strange I feel this need for a change. In the middle of all that "change" is my face, quizzical and far from flattered. *Dis*flattered—is that a word? Probably not, but a fit description.

I hide out in the restroom as long as I reasonably can, but I can guess what is coming. I decide it is best to get it over with.

Once back in the gathering room, Collin tries to catch my attention through the entire poetry reading. I stare straight ahead, listening to Mariah. She is reading a few lilting Shakespeare sonnets. And Collin is reading way too much into them. He is thinking I walk in beauty like the night. I swear I can read his mind.

Collin appears beside me. Somehow he has inched his way over. "Liz," Collin whispers too loudly. A few heads turn toward us, but he does not seem to notice. "I'd like to take you to dinner after work today."

There it is.

Mariah finishes. We clap and the crowd begins to move toward the food.

"I hear you're not seeing anyone," says Collin. "It's perfect weather. Let's go for dinner and a nice walk in the moonlight."

I am resolved. "While I thank you for your invitation, I must decline it."

His face, amused, tells me I will not get off that easily.

"You wish to hold out and increase my interest. You've done this before, so it's not a surprise."

"Really, Collin. This is a *no*. A real no."

"Women and their little games." He wags his finger at me playfully. His face is like a little child's. "I never need to see the sun again, Liz, because your eyes light up my world."

I feel so unkind, but proceed. Deep breath. "I'm not interested in you. That's as plain as I can put it. I don't want to go out with you again."

Collin's shiny eyes dull. I can see my words cutting into his soul. He looks about the room where a few people are leaning in, listening to our conversation.

"I'm sorry," I say. It sounds so weak.

Collin suddenly wants to leave. I would too. He seems a bit lost, as though he is not sure where he is. He begins to plod to the exit.

Charlotte, coming up behind me, says, "Oh, dear, Liz. That poor guy."

"I had no choice." I look around the room. "Let's enjoy the afternoon, if we can."

Charlotte's eyes are still fixed on Collin. "I'll get him some treats. That will maybe cheer him up."

She places a few petit fours on a plate and carries them toward Collin. Charlotte is so sweet that way. A real giver.

I do not feel like eating after all. I sit down and listen for ten minutes to Mrs. Bennet lecture me on how cruel I was for leading Collin on.

Another rainy afternoon. A soft bed. Another game of "musical books" with Mrs. Hill.

Ten Little Indians is open before me. I am draped across the bed on my stomach, propped up on my elbows. A little rain is all the excuse I need to read, nap, read all day.

How Agatha Christie managed to write this book, I wish I knew. It is that pure genius page-turner that puts most other mystery novels to shame.

An eclectic group of ten people are invited to Soldier Island. All of them are guilty of murder or manslaughter, but somehow escaped punishment. A gramophone announces they will soon all pay for their crimes.

And a character named Anthony is poisoned immediately.

I sit up straighter, my mind racing with what I know, trying to guess the murderer, however improbable that is at this point. My finger readies to flip the page and. . .

A warm, heavy cat body plops onto the book and pins my hand down. Mrs. Hill twitches her tail and purrs. *Meow.*

"You understand I'm reading this one?" I wiggle my hand out from underneath her.

She looks at me as though she understands, but cares not the least bit.

I try to placate her: scratch her back, sing her praises, give her that attention she is aiming for. Then I make the mistake of trying to slip the book out from under her. She narrows her eyes and hisses at me.

Fine, kitty. I can multi-task. I can read two books at the same time.

Bookshelf scan. Ahh. *The Martian.* Nothing like a bit of sci-fi to balance out all the murder. Besides, Matt Damon is on the cover. Meow.

Now I am stuck on Mars. My crew believes I am dead and has abandoned me in the middle of a sandstorm. How will I eat? How will I let NASA know I am alive?

I get instantly locked into the book. I do not even notice, until far too late, the fuzzy shadow creeping across the bed.

And, *plop*—cat body on book.

Okay. *Indians* is free. Switch. Left side of the bed.

Another murder; this time the victim "overslept." More suspicions and heightened panic.

Switch. Right side of the bed.

I am growing potatoes. Colonizing Mars. Dang, Matt

Damon/Mark Watney, you are a resourceful guy.

Wait—how can there be "life" on Mars if there are no books there?

And, *cat on book*.

Mrs. Hill! How did I not see that coming?

I need a decoy book. Something unreadable. No—not unreadable as in the headache-inducing *Ulysses* or the indecipherable *Voynich Manuscript*. I am thinking "something-so-terribly-written-I-don't-mind-if-my-cat-puts-her-butt-on-it" tripe.

There. Bottom of the pile on my nightstand: *Twilight*.

Book out and open.

Waiting. Pretending to read *Twilight* while attempting to peek across the bed at *Indians*. But I cannot turn the page without giving myself away.

Mrs. Hill stares at me without blinking. *She knows.*

Another murder occurs before Mrs. Hill attempts to sit on *Indians*.

This time I am the one who hisses. I flip onto my back and hold *Ten Little Indians* as far in the air as I can and still manage to read.

Even then, a paw reaches out and swipes at the pages.

When it rains, it pours. In more ways than one.

The ground is nothing but mud thanks to our unusually heavy rains of late. I put my little truck into gear and the tires flip mud all over my neighbor's car as I back out onto the road. I am already running late for work, thanks to my ridiculous indecision over clothing: I tried on six outfits before one felt right. Now I need to make every second count and my ineffectual tires do not know it.

The rain starts pounding the windshield and I struggle to see the road. A nearby ditch is overflowing and leaving the road extra slippery. My truck starts to fishtail across the expanse of the road. I feel a gut-wrenching *thud*.

My truck tire is in the ditch. I put the truck into 4-wheel drive, but it does not have enough pull to get out. I make several attempts to get my tire unstuck, grinding the wheels into the ground. However, this only mixes the dirt in with the rainwater more.

Screw it. I can walk to work.

I call Jane. "Do you have any extra clothes with you?"

"Uh, oh. That doesn't sound good. I've just got some gym shorts and a T-shirt."

"Those will have to do. I'll explain later."

I hang up and I hop out of the truck straight into a mud puddle I thought would be shallow. Boy, was I wrong. My carefully-selected red skirt and black blouse take an immediate hit from the splash. I nearly lose a sandal.

The road into town seems interminable as I hobble along, rain drizzling over me, mud squishing out between my toes. When I took the apartment attached to a farmhouse out in the boonies, I did it for the superb view of the fields and hills surrounding Hertford. I am learning that perfection has its price. There is a mile before the edge of town and a mile of town pavement to walk.

The clouds suddenly roll away as though the whole thing was a joke. A touch of sunshine beams down on me, too late to do any good.

I pass a large road sign advertising The Potato Museum. "Free taters for out-of-staters!" it says next to an enormous baked potato topped with sour cream. I wonder how many of the visiting Californians ever took up the offer of a free "tater."

Two locals stop to give me a ride, but I wave them on. The looks on their faces tell me I am tough on the eyes. The wind makes sure my hair is frizzled and uncommitted to its original style. Longbourn Library just has to accept what it gets.

At long last, I walk into the library.

"Dear child!" Mrs. Bennet shouts when she sees me. "You're *filthy!*"

"Long story. Jane, where are those clothes?"

She hands them to me with her mouth open.

I try heading toward the bathroom to change, but the long skirt is heavy with mud. I kick off one slippery sandal and hike up my skirt enough to get the other one. That is when I notice I have an audience.

Of *course* Darcy is standing there. He is mortified.

"Liz?" he asks, as though he is not sure it is me. "Are you *okay?*"

I give him my best smile, balancing on one foot. I am not going to let the cretin think I cannot handle a little mud. "Perfectly."

Then I lose my balance.

In a flash, my body is careening toward the floor, but I do not get there. I suddenly find myself instead suspended in the air, clutching Darcy's shoulder.

I blink a few times. Darcy's arm is solid around me. His face is way too close to mine.

I quickly establish my footing and push away from him. I step back. Phew. "Thank you, Mr. Darcy. Those are some lightning reflexes you have there."

"You're welcome," he says, then bends down to gather Jane's clothes I dropped. I take them with my one semi-clean hand and go through the problematic motions of thanking him again.

I see I left some token mud on his suit. I point to it. "Sorry," I say, then try to wipe it off. Instead, I leave another smudge. Ugh.

"Maybe. . .*you* should get that?" I suggest.

Darcy looks down to analyze the smudges. He is underwhelmed. "Before you make it worse?"

Is that a little smile? Surely he's laughing at me.

"Perhaps," I reply. "If you'll excuse me, Mr. Darcy." I make a beeline to the restroom.

That was awkward, to say the least. Another bizarre moment in my already bizarre day. A sense of déjà vu nags me, as though I have just acted out a scene from a book I have read before. I cannot place the book, though, and shake off the notion.

Once inside the bathroom I look in the mirror. It is far worse than I had imagined. Mud splatters dot a path all the way up to my face. A hem six inches deep in mud. Hair that cannot be called hair. Apparently, it is an early Halloween here at Longbourn Library. And a fastidious man in a perfectly tailored suit just *had* to witness it.

I clean up as best I can and speed-dial Jed, the tow truck guy.

There are a rather large number of people visiting the library today. It is a Friday afternoon before a three-day weekend. Everyone seems to be checking out stacks of DVDs. A few are getting handfuls of books.

Mrs. Young informs me I must sit behind the checkout desk all day due to the length of Jane's gym shorts. My sink-washed hair is pulled into a ponytail. The T-shirt I am wearing screams "Exercise is my natural high." I feel like a hypocrite since I have not been to a gym in months.

Darcy, now with no discernible trace of mud on his suit, has been here for over an hour. He sits at the table closest to the checkout desk. Already his next ten books are stacked in front of him. He flips through one, but he keeps looking up at the checkout line.

I wonder why Darcy does not just get in line and check his books out already. He starts pacing around the library. I watch his suit go back and forth, back and forth. Is he upset about something? His face seems concerned and focused. Finally, when Jane rushes off to help someone find a book about delivering calves, Darcy approaches the checkout desk.

"Have you been to Sacramento?" Darcy asks me. His brown eyes concentrate keenly on my face.

I am thrown for a loop. This conversation has no segue, and I cannot read the expression on his face.

"Umm, I drove through it once. Well, my *father* did the driving, actually. We made a long scenic trip to Disneyland when I was a child, but that's the only time I've been to the west coast."

Memories of California briefly flash through my mind: shorts, tank tops, bleach-blonde hair. Funny, I do not remember seeing a great quantity of tailored suits. Or sideburns, for that matter.

Darcy continues, "Are you attached to Idaho?"

"Well, *yes*. You could say that. I grew up here. My father is here." I am on some surreal planet, wondering why I am talking about these things at all.

Darcy considers. "But California is an easy distance away, wouldn't you say?"

Huh? "I *suppose*, if one can afford plane tickets." That is something I am sure he does not worry about.

"True. True."

I point to his stack of books. "Would you like me to check those out by telepathy?"

Half a smile from him. "No. Here."

I input his books into the system. He watches each movement carefully. Done.

I hold out Darcy's checkout slip. He reaches for the slip, taking my fingers in hand with it. He looks down, surprised by his blunder.

"Pardon," he says, releasing my fingers. He looks away in embarrassment.

I pull my hand back swiftly. "Excuse me, Mr. Darcy, I need those fingers. Have a nice day."

But still he lingers.

Hmm. "Can I help you with anything else, Mr. Darcy?"

He is nervous. Did I say something to offend him?

"No. Not today, I think. Bye." And suddenly he is gone, barely remembering to take his ten books with him.

Jane comes back to the desk, a perplexed look straining her face. "Liz, what have you done to Darcy?"

Who knows what is going on in the mind of that stuffed shirt? "I have no idea. Absolutely no clue."

Chapter 7

They are all gathered around the checkout desk when I arrive for my afternoon shift: Kitty, Lydia, Jane, Mary, and Mrs. Bennet. The looks on their faces are solemn.

"Tell me the ugly news," I say. "Just get it over with."

They exchange glances, asking each other tacitly to express the inexpressible.

Kitty finds the courage. "You recall that night you snubbed Collin."

Mrs. Bennet sniffs.

"Of course. That was barely more than a week ago."

"Well," says Jane carefully. "You remember that Collin met Charlotte?"

Instantly, my mind starts racing, choosing from dozens of awful scenarios. "Oh, no. Is he *stalking* her? Did he *murder* her? What. . ."

Jane shakes her head.

Mrs. Bennet bursts out, "They're *engaged!*"

My legs suddenly lose their stability. "Collin and my dear friend *Charlotte*? Impossible."

Kitty says, "It's true. We heard it from Kate de Bourgh herself."

Jane emphasizes, "*None* of us saw this coming, Liz. Don't be too hard on yourself."

"*I* saw it coming," Mrs. Bennet explains with a huff. "If you die an old maid, Liz, you can't blame me. I did everything in my power to get you and Collin together."

Lydia laughs and snorts.

My mind is so loud, it drowns out Mrs. Bennet's further chastisements. *How* could this have happened? Am I somehow to blame? *Charlotte?* My brain cannot process such a foreign concept. I need to hear it from the source herself.

"Excuse me," I say, interrupting Mrs. Bennet mid-sentence. I sprint to The Brink Room and pull out my phone.

I dial.

The instant Charlotte picks up, she says, "We can't all afford to be romantic, Liz."

"Dad, the world is completely skewampus and it is all my fault," I agonize over the phone.

My father is laughing, but I am not trying to be entertaining.

"Really, Dad. Accept it. If I hadn't rejected Collin right there, Charlotte would not have felt sorry for him and *fed* him. Then this whole horror story would not exist. Oh, my gosh, I can't believe she's going to *marry him*!"

"Are they happy?"

"They're both too clueless not to be." I start petting Mrs. Hill's head too hard. She purrs for a few seconds, then swipes at me.

"Let it go, then," my father says. "Happy is happy. What is wrong with that?"

I push Mrs. Hill off my lap. "It's not. . .it's not *romance*. It's not *enough*."

"It's not enough for *you*, Lizzie. Don't project your expectations onto them. You'll make yourself miserable. Not everyone gets a fairy tale romance."

"I suppose you're right," I decide. "Most of us ache for that love we read about, but it isn't realistic. There is no Elinor Dashwood and Edward Ferrars, no Heathcliff and Cathy, no Robin Hood and Maid Marian. Love stories just build up our expectations before a crashing fall. In the end, the prince often turns out to be a charmless wonder or the princess runs off with a truck driver."

My father sighs. "Now you're being too pessimistic."

"Sorry," I try to compose myself. "Especially for the bit about the truck driver."

"Love you, Lizzie. Sleep it off."

"Love you back. Okay, I will."

I sit towards the back of the lecture hall, excited for William Fitz's reading. The venue is abuzz with literary conversation. Hands everywhere clutch copies of *Pemberley*. Two women slide past me.

"What does he look like?" one woman says to another, breathless and elated.

I scan the room. There is one stunning gentleman standing toward the front. He is tall, blond, and apparently carved by Michelangelo. I hope that is William Fitz. I slip into a fantasy where we meet and one thing leads to another. How quickly my imagination jumps from admiration to love, from love to matrimony. In my mind, we are just setting a wedding date when I stop cold.

Darcy. He is sitting so close to the podium that William Fitz is going to spit on him during the reading. That California haircut and sideburns. His unmistakable precise ensemble. It all just ruined my fantasy.

Mary walks in and sits resolutely next to me. She has already pointed out to me some potential inaccuracies in the historical context of *Pemberley*. I wonder if she is here for a reading or to corner a hapless author. She is a force to be reckoned with.

Kate de Bourgh's daughter Anne is sitting in the corner of the second row. Her face is pale and detached. She sits limply, barely moving her head to acknowledge the other people in the room. She would blend right into the wall if it were not for the stylish pink wrap she is wearing. Though I have never seen Anne take an interest in Darcy, rumors abound that her mother imagines a romance there. A black suit and a pink wrap. They would make a proper couple.

Kate de Bourgh sashays to the podium and asks everyone to sit down. Her hair is done up in a turban as though she came here directly from a 1930's movie shoot. She declares, "If I'd ever learned to write, I would have been a *great* author. Instead, I have the privilege of introducing one to you."

Then she rambles for five minutes, mostly about herself. Apparently, she never learned to *read*, either. She appears to believe Pemberley is a man's name. The more she prattles, the more I cringe. Finally, she says, "Now, let's hear from the man himself. William Fitz, would you stand up, please."

I stop breathing. And forget to start again.

Oh, holy flip. It is *Darcy*.

Well, evidently I did remember to breathe again. I am still alive. But not myself.

Darcy reads, "Pemberley was a large, handsome, stone building, standing well on rising ground, and backed by a ridge of high woody hills; and in front, a stream of some natural importance was swelled into greater, but without any artificial appearance. Its banks were neither formal, nor falsely adorned. . ."

Though Darcy's reading is flat, almost stoic, the words of *Pemberley* fill my senses and I am transported back into that beloved book. Darcy, obviously nervous, has a delicious though quivering resonance to his voice that enriches the story. It never occurred to me in the midst of all those jokes about underwear that Darcy is a *real* writer and not just some wannabe or that he would use a pseudonym like William Fitz.

Darcy looks about the room as he reads. At one point, I catch his eye and he abruptly pauses in the middle of his sentence.

I cannot read his expression precisely—it is surprise and relief in a few seconds of thoughtful focus. I see a flash of what I think is a smile.

Darcy places a finger on the page, then goes back to reading, suddenly more comfortable in his own skin. His courage rises. The words flow better. For several more minutes, the audience is suspended in the world of *Pemberley*, each person considering it from their own perspective as though it were a Rembrandt in an art gallery. No one is moving, just appreciating.

I know I would be happy if Darcy read the book in its entirety. I could sit all day in this moment, feeling nothing but the spiral of imagination circulating about in my mind. I could steal away into *Pemberley* and never look back.

The reading concludes with a standing ovation.

For the Q & A session, Kate de Bourgh requests a few questions from the audience. I try to come up with some good questions, but all I can think of is "How could *you* write *Pemberley*, you preening butthead?"

And, I decide it is best to keep my hand down.

The first few questions are mostly about characters—motivations for their actions, displeasure over their getting killed off, and so on. Darcy answers each question with an unexpected smoothness. He is polite, even when it is clear a question is critical.

I am horrified to see Mary raise her hand. "Really, Mary, this is hardly the time," I whisper. My face is in my hands, waiting for the bomb to drop.

She stands and asks, "Did you have a particular estate in mind when you wrote the details of *Pemberley*?"

Oh. That was remarkably normal.

Darcy replies, "I once made a visit to the gorgeous Lyme Park in Cheshire, England. That became my main inspiration for *Pemberley*. It was an estate I imagined a family would be willing to fight for."

I have seen pictures of that stately home. It is the stuff of dreams. The next best thing to a castle to share with a prince.

"One final question," says Kate de Bourgh.

A skinny redhead in the middle of the room raises her hand.

"Okay, miss."

She stands up and coyly asks, "Umm. Are you single?"

The crowd laughs. I gag.

Darcy seems to be blushing, if that is possible. "Currently, yes. But I hope not for long."

A ripple of giggles spreads through the room. The redhead collapses into her chair in a fit of twitterpation. Oh, brother. He has a groupie already.

Kate de Bourgh is beaming. She looks over at her daughter and gives her a discreet thumbs-up. Anne does not seem to move a muscle.

Most of the crowd gets in line to get their copies of *Pemberley* signed. I look at the length of the line and decide to wait. Mary simply pushes her way to the front.

It is then I notice *him*. John Wickham himself, mixed in with all those readers.

"Hey!" I say to him. Not my smoothest moment. I am always much more articulate in my head than in real life.

"Hey, yourself." He grins and it is supremely gorgeous.

"Are you a *Pemberley* fan?" I ask. Oh, gosh. Of course he is. Why else would he be here?

He takes a thoughtful pause. "You could say that."

"Do you have a book to sign?" I could not see one.

"No. I just want to have a talk with the author."

"Do you know Darcy?"

"Yes. We were roommates in college, actually."

"What an amazing coincidence. Are you from Sacramento?"

"I'm from here. But, my father helped his parents find their summer house here in Hertford years ago. Long story short, that's how we became acquainted and later became roommates at Cal State."

"Extraordinary. Does he know you're here?"

"No." He seems embarrassed. "This is entirely a surprise."

"Nice. Oh, the line's moving."

"See you later, lovely Liz."

Sigh. Be still my heart.

John is garrulous as he interacts with those around him. He laughs his way up the line. I see Darcy bristle at the sound of John's laugh. Darcy looks up from signing one book, sees John. Darcy's face goes cold and hard.

The room is noisy and I cannot make out what John and Darcy are saying to each other. John reaches out his hand for Darcy to shake. Darcy stands up and waves John away. He is upset, nearly livid with John.

John, without losing an ounce of composure, holds up his hands as if surrendering, then turns. He slides through the crowd toward the exit.

Huh???

I am a mix of emotions. Highs and lows. Uncertainty. The line goes on and on. I decide to get my copy of *Pemberley* signed another time.

I take my exit.

Chapter 8

John is sitting on the hood of his Buick in the parking lot. The way he is hunched, he looks like a little boy, an Oliver Twist who was just denied a bowl of soup.

I cannot help it. "It is not my business, but it seems like the reunion didn't go so well."

John looks down at his hand, the one Darcy refused to shake. "Yes, I imagined things differently."

"Darcy is a bit formal and severe, but I've never seen him be flat out rude to anyone. Now I wonder how he has any friends at all."

"Sounds like you know him well."

"We're acquainted. He comes to the library once a week, maybe."

He brightens. "You work at the library?"

"Guilty."

He smiles. "So you've got both brains and looks. That's a rare combination."

"If you came to the library, you wouldn't say so. Well, unless you saw *Mary*." I quickly cover my mouth with my hand. "Did I just say that?"

"Who's being rude now?" He laughs heartily.

"Oh, no." I am turning red.

"It's okay," he gets out after his laughter dies. "I really needed that after my little humiliation in there." His dimples grow. "Actually, I could use a piece of pie. Do you like pie?"

"Is it chocolate?"

"It can be."

"Then I say yes."

We meet at Pie in the Sky. Along the restaurant wall is a small bookshelf with maybe twenty books on it. John picks up *The Idiot*.

John examines the thick book and says, "That's an awfully long book to explain something so simple. 'The man is stupid.' That's all it needs to say."

"Do you write for CliffsNotes?"

"It's one of my many jobs. I'd be happy to summarize any book you'd like," he offers.

"I've read all of these. No summary needed."

"Of course," he laughs. "I forgot who I was talking to: The Great Reader."

"I'm not a 'great reader' per se, but I sure enjoy a good book. Pie?" I point to the nearest booth.

"*Pie.*"

Soon he is eating the boysenberry pie introspectively. I am thinking about the abrupt and outrageous way Darcy brushed John off.

I down a few bites of chocolate silk pie before I venture, "Tell me what you think happened at the reading."

John looks at me with a purposeful intensity; his voice drops to a low timbre. "You may have noticed Darcy's anxiety when I tried to talk to him. He clearly did not want to see me there." He stabs at his pie. "That's because I know his secret."

He pauses, looks around the room as though someone may be listening. The secret hangs in the air between us.

John lowers his voice further. "Darcy knows that he stole my book and passed it off as his own."

"He *what*?!" I drop my next forkful of pie.

"*Pemberley*. I wrote the manuscript by hand over several years while I was in college. I kept my only copy locked in a briefcase next to my bed. One day, it was missing. The whole briefcase. Three years later, I heard Darcy had published a book under a pseudonym. When I bought a copy, I knew what happened to my manuscript."

I am floored. For the second time tonight, I forget to breathe for several seconds. I never cared much for Darcy, but could he really be *this bad*?

"I don't know why I'm telling you this," John continues, playing with his pie. He gives me a look of vulnerable trust. "I forgave him quite a long time ago. I was hoping I could come here today and Darcy and I could put the past behind us."

"But *Pemberley* is so successful! He is bound to make a fortune on it! How could that not upset you?"

"He was like my brother at one time. I can't forget that. It's true I struggle with money now, but I try not to hold it against him."

Anger boils up. "Darcy deserves to be publicly disgraced for what he's done."

"He will one day, but not by me." John considers, "I suppose I just don't have the resentful character that some men have."

"You're a good soul, John. Better than most."

"Thank you." He reaches across the table and squeezes my hand.

So, John is the genius. He is the writer and Darcy is even more of a jerk than I thought he was in the beginning. But worse. Darcy is not just an arrogant peacock; he is a thief. A sneak. A plagiarizer.

My heart sinks.

"I hope Darcy's visits to the library will not deter you from coming in."

"Not at all. If he wishes to avoid seeing me, he must be the one to stay away from the library. I will come soon, I promise."

I look forward to his keeping that promise. Before we separate, I invite John to the next Tuesday Tea.

I do not sleep well that night. I just toss and turn, oscillating between anger and disgust at Darcy.

Mrs. Hill assumes I am awake so I can pet her. She cuddles up to me while I seethe.

The next day at work, I can barely keep my eyes open. I am grumbly and off-balance. Before the first patrons arrive, the whole story spills out to Jane.

"There must be some sort of misunderstanding," Jane says.

"Jane, you can't think poorly of anyone, can you."

"The facts in this case are unverified." Her expression conveys her doubts.

"John seemed so *sincere*. He put the matter in such a way I couldn't help but believe him. I keep thinking of my first impression of Darcy. This situation only confirms my conclusions about him." My contempt is hard to hide.

"I am on your side, no matter what," Jane tells me. Those are the words of a loyal woman who does not want to think poorly of her crush's best friend.

I do not want to push my hurt and ugly feelings onto such a person. I drop the matter and start the slow crawl through my work day.

I care too much. It is one of my many "virtues." *Why is it that my fate is to see everything and take it all so much to heart?* I ask myself, evoking Lara from *Dr. Zhivago*. My heart is in a slump. I cannot pinpoint the magic I usually find in my job.

And, I wish I could not eavesdrop so easily in the library. People forget that a simple bookshelf does not stop the sound of their voices. I am locating Elizabeth Gaskell's *North and South* while Kate de Bourgh is concluding her meeting with Mrs. Young.

As she exits The Brink Room, Kate says, "These *Idaho* girls. Can you imagine one thinking she had a *chance* with Charles Bingley? I don't know the particulars, but I heard Darcy say that he sent Charles away on account of it. He made him take a job offer in New York. . ."

Darcy just gets worse and worse. *Shameful scoundrel.*

I hold onto the bookshelf to compose myself. I want to smack something. No, I want to smack *someone*. HIM.

I think of Jane sitting at the checkout desk, oblivious to what I just heard. She is all loveliness and goodness—twice the woman I will ever be. Who could possibly object to such a picture of perfection?

I know *exactly* who: a proud, frigid jerk named *Will Darcy*.

Chapter 9

One of the big summer events every year is the Summer Scavenger Hunt, which is part of our summer reading program. This is a way for kids to practice finding books in the library and compete like animals for prizes. Roughly thirty children and some of their parents have shown up. Kitty has the kids divided into groups of three. Each group has a list of 12 categories to find: *1) a book with a potato in it, 2) a book about the Lewis and Clark expedition, 3) a book about Yellowstone,* and so on.

The adults are not allowed to help the children. The kids use the database, their own knowledge of books, good old-fashioned page-flipping, and, occasionally, *stealing*. The best part is when the children want to check out the books they have discovered in the process. It always gets rough and rowdy. And, yes, it is a nightmare to clean up after.

"Ready? Go!!" shouts Kitty.

Scramble, scramble, squeal. No Mr. Bennet here today.

Thirty minutes of disorder. Children everywhere. Pushing and arguing. Dropping books. *Crying.*

The first potential winners bring their stack of books for inspection, but I send them back for a book that features the Rocky Mountains.

Another group emerges, led by a confident little boy.

"We saw that book *first!*" a little girl from another group screams at the boy.

The Enormous Potato suddenly gets caught in a tug-of-war.

"We *touched* it first!" the boy screams back.

I tell the girl, "There are LOTS of books to choose from. If he touched the book first, it's his. Keep looking." She scowls at me, then shoves the book back at the boy.

Mary comes over, almost eager to intervene. "We must stem the tide of malice and pour into each other's bosoms the balm of consolation."

The boy's face goes blank. He considers what he just heard. "Mom!" he calls to a woman hanging nearby. "This woman said *bosoms*. You said that's a bad word."

The mother shoots Mary a scathing look.

Mary, affronted at the accusation of doing anything inappropriate, slinks back to the reference desk.

I finish inspecting the stack of books. We have our 1st place winners.

The winning group struts out with ribbons, Amazon gift cards, and decent-sized stacks of books. At least the winners are happy. The ones who come in at a lower rank are disappointed, angry even.

My nerves are frazzled from lack of sleep and the horrid revelations from two days ago. I watch the clock, but it seems to be going at half-pace. Three more hours to go.

A patron sent in a hold request for *The Book Thief*. It is nearly closing time. I go to the Z section on the last shelf in the corner, perusing for *Zusak*.

I hear: "You left so early the other night."

Oh, no. Darcy's very presence gives me shudders. He is standing in my way.

"I had to."

"Did you enjoy the book?"

"*Pemberley*?" I do not want to sound too enthusiastic about his plagiarized book. "It is good, I suppose."

"I'm glad you approve of it."

I am too tired for politeness and just nauseated I have to pretend right now. "Excuse me. I have to get back to work."

Darcy stands there unmoved, his breathing quickened. After a few uncertain, uncomfortable moments, he blurts out, "I want to go out with you. I can't help it."

I take a step back. Did I hear that right?

He fidgets at my open-mouthed stare, but continues. "I can't struggle with this anymore. You're not the kind of woman I usually date, I realize. You're a bit unsophisticated, among other things. But, I'm willing to put those issues aside and give you a chance."

I am incredulous. *Unsophisticated*? He will give *me* a chance? I feel tears brewing, but this only angers me more.

"No. I won't go out with you."

There it is on his face, as though I slapped him: confusion, then pain. His face goes a shade paler. Several heavy seconds follow.

"Is that all I can expect? A flat rejection?" he whispers, quite stunned.

I hate that I have to defend myself. "If you want reasons, I can give you reasons."

Darcy is clearly unprepared for this unfathomable situation. He considers and says, "Okay. I'd like to know why it's so easy for you to dismiss me."

"As though pointing out I'm an inferior choice isn't enough?

How could I agree to go out with you after that? I would have to concede in some way that you're right, and I can't."

He starts to pace. He is not used to chastisement, I am sure. Whatever pity I might have for him is absent as I see him squirm in that suit.

I keep going, too tired to hold back. I lower my voice so Jane will not be able to hear this part. "While I'm at it—where is Charlie, sir? Why did he leave so suddenly and without saying goodbye? You *sent* him away, didn't you? I learned you tried to separate him from Jane. We're talking about two people who were *perfect* for each other. Was it really so hard for you to believe they'd be happy together?"

He stops and faces me. "I detected no real feelings on her side."

"Jane holds back a lot, but her true friends had no doubt about her feelings for him."

"Charlie gets distracted from the important things. He has always been that way. I was worried his attentions to Jane would derail him from his career. A librarian is hardly what his parents expect him to bring home."

"She was *falling in love with him*." My voice rises. "If her heart is broken, his must be too."

Darcy looks away. He starts pacing again.

"There's more." My voice is vitriolic. "You've done something else that I could never turn a blind eye to." I have a hard time saying the words. "You stole John Wickham's book and passed it off as your own!"

Mary shushes me from the other side of the shelves.

Darcy halts his pacing and faces me. "I did *what*?!"

"You heard me. The secret is out. John Wickham—he told me all about it. You, who hardly need the money or attention while he's struggling to get by in real estate. Oh, it's unconscionable, despicable, and. . ." I cannot think of the right word. ". . .just *monstrous*! You're the last man in this world I could possibly date."

"Ssshhhh. *Sshhhhhhhhhhh*," Mary hisses again.

Oh, bite me, Mary.

"I. . ." Darcy is genuinely flummoxed. His sideburns look lopsided. "So, this is your opinion of me? Of course your answer is no."

I cross my arms. I am not backing down.

Darcy is unglued, but still makes an effort to appear gentlemanly. "Sorry for taking up your time, Ms. Liz."

He marches out the doors of Longbourn Library.

Farewell, prick.

Chapter 10

First thing the next morning, the man I want most to forget startles me as I am unlocking the library. I instinctively wrap my fingers around the can of Mace in my pocket.

Darcy holds out an envelope.

"Ms. Liz, please do me the honor of reading this letter," he says in a soft, pleasing manner. His eyes are bloodshot and his hair, for once, unkempt.

A strain of pity on my part causes me to drop the Mace and reach for the letter. Darcy leaves so quickly, I stand there in the morning sunlight and question if he had really even been there.

I slip the letter into my purse and start my work day. A new surge of anger takes over me. I *do not* want to know what Darcy has to say. That stuck-up lout stole John's manuscript. He sent Charlie away from Jane. And, of course, he *completely insulted* me by asking me out! I agree with Mrs. Bennet—the *nerve* of that man!

I find myself pressing computer keys extra hard and slapping books into patrons' hands as though they were to blame for what I am feeling. Everything I do is uncivil. *This isn't me, this isn't me,* I repeat to myself. I nearly start to cry again, but remind myself that I did enough of that last night.

Why is the clock moving so slowly? The sheer weight of emotion keeps me dragging.

Jane is concerned. "Go home, Liz. I'll stay a little longer to cover you."

"I'm fine," I say, but not with any real conviction.

"Go."

Mary pontificates, "A friend in need is a friend indeed."

"Thank you, Mary," Jane offers.

I feel weak for doing it, but I need not to be at work too. "Thank you. You know I love you, Jane?"

"Of course. Now, leave."

I wait until I get home to take the letter in my hands. Darcy is going to try to change my mind and I do not want it to change. I just want to be right so I can hate him. I slowly open the envelope and unfold the gold-foil-trimmed letter. Deep breath.

The letter reads:

Dear Ms. Liz,

Based on what you believe I have done, I cannot blame you for your antipathy toward me. Please allow me a chance to clear my name. I will not attempt to renew any sentiments that you clearly find so disgusting.

First, John Wickham is a snake. He was my roommate in grad school during his spotty academic career. During that time, I watched him deceive and manipulate people whenever it suited him. More than once I found him wearing an army uniform in a bar, using this ruse to pick up women. He would tell people all kinds of sob stories so they would give him money, which he promptly spent on his frequent trips to Reno. I also made the mistake of lending him money from time to time, never to see a cent returned.

I tolerated him because he had deceived me, too, into thinking we were good friends. Meanwhile, he was working his *lowest and most despicable scam on my sister, Georgiana. They met during one of her visits. She was only 17 at the time. He got her number off my phone and initiated a secret relationship with her. John wooed my sister with poetry he told her he wrote, but obviously he had borrowed from an old book. She soon believed herself to be in love. She bought every lie he told her. He promised her they would run away together on her 18th birthday. He convinced her he just needed some money to get his writing career off the ground first. She gave him nearly all her savings before I discovered what was going on.*

You can imagine what I felt and how I acted toward John. I demanded he return the money, but he had already gambled it all away. He was already failing college, so he just left California entirely. My dear sister was simply abandoned with a lesson in reality that left her both broke and brokenhearted.

Now John is here, apparently claiming to be a real estate agent. Try looking up his name in the real estate listings. He is not there. Once again, he is up to his old tricks, trying to find people to exploit. I am not surprised he claims my book is his. He will use every chance he can to besmirch my name. It is perfect retaliation for getting him away from my sister. Test him sometime. He could not write a decent postcard. He relies on deceit and will continue to as long as he has an audience. I am sincerely sorry he has been conning you, Liz, of all people.

I put the letter down at this point. Can it be true? *John*? John seems so smooth, so appealing, so *perfect*.

Most sociopaths do, I suppose.

Whom do I believe? If Darcy is telling the truth, it would certainly explain his behavior the night of the reading. I would not blame him for his abrasiveness, either. I would be guilty of the same, or worse, if someone hurt someone I love that much. I keep reading.

Second, you were right that I encouraged Charlie to pursue his career in New York. I did everything in my power to separate him from Jane. His family has always pressured him to make something of himself. And, though he has found some success as a stockbroker, he could not possibly be the star they want him to be. Not here in Idaho. He needed to be learning from the best on Wall Street. I saw the way Charlie looked at Jane and worried he would throw his chance at this job away over a flirtation. I convinced him, as I believed it was true, that she was not so attached to him. I did it for his own good, and as a friend.

Once again, I apologize for the way I made you uncomfortable.

Yours,

Will Darcy

I feel like I just got off a roller coaster. I am disoriented, but inwardly satisfied. I cannot help it: I think Darcy might be right about John. I think of how John could not get me into the little blue house. It easily could have been an act.

As for Jane's situation, I cannot find it in my heart, not yet, to forgive him for destroying all Jane's hope of happiness, however well-intentioned his motives. I am grateful to have some facts—and I truly hope they are *facts* this time—to help me judge the situation with a clearer mind.

Mrs. Hill sits down on the letter. She rolls her ginger body around on it and bites a corner off.

"You go, girl," I tell her.

She is in one of her "crazy" moods, no doubt set off by my insanity the last few days. She runs back and forth from the kitchen to the living room, turning in circles and meowing bizarrely. She does this until she is exhausted.

We stay up late watching a Colin Firth movie and eating ice cream. The next day, a blessed Sunday, we both feel a lot better.

"Darcy asked you out last week? And you're only now telling me about it? I never would have seen that one coming," Jane tells me. She has to sit down to think about it. "He's always so *severe* and cold; I didn't think he had a romantic feeling in him. What was your answer?"

"It was a no. A very firm no. I've never been so harsh in my life."

"Well, it explains your, ummm, *agitation* on Saturday. Poor Darcy."

I pause for a moment to input Mrs. Phillips's weekly stack of gardening books, plus the bodice-ripper she snuck into her pile. As tacitly implied, I act as though I did not notice the off-topic book.

I continue, "Really, Jane, I can't feel much compassion for Darcy. I have no doubt his pride will drive away any feelings he has for me."

"Well, there's always a handsome guy named John Wickham. He stopped by Saturday and asked to see you, but you'd already left."

"*That* book is closed too. For now."

"That's surprising. You've always spoken so warmly of him."

"I heard some things, let's say. John may not be what he seems."

"There's such an expression of *goodness* in his demeanor. I don't know what you could have unearthed."

"I just want to verify the facts before I let you know."

"That's good of you. I doubt I'd believe anything bad you would say about John, anyway."

Men such as John, if Darcy is correct, count on that appearance of goodness. The charm could well be nothing but slight-of-hand, an illusion.

My mind goes back and forth, managing the different scenarios from every angle. It is still hard for me to believe John could be anything but what he presents.

"I have organized them according to ethical and theological relevance in our day and age," says Mary as she presents me with her display of children's books. She is quite pleased with herself.

The books are lined up like soldiers, standing straight up and marked with sticky notes. They fill a whole table.

Lydia usually makes an oversimplified display of books by color or size. Kitty may do something with fairy tales or holidays. Jane often does classical and historical themes. But this is what you get when you ask Mary to design and organize a display for children: *Tom Brown's Schooldays*, *The Wouldbegoods*, *The History of Little Goody Two Shoes*, Sarah Fielding's *The Governess*, *Fordyce's Sermons*, and so on. I know for a fact *The Children's Book of Virtues* is the only one on the table written in the past 100 years. Most of the books are didactic, patronizing, and overtly sexist.

Are *these* the books Mary's parents read to her as a child?

She explains, "I recommend the children read them in order, starting with *Tom Brown's Schooldays*. They should pay *particular attention* to the passages I have marked. If they read every day, they can finish all of them by the end of the month. I will type up specific instructions to include with the display."

"This display will generate some interesting comments," I say. I realize the words *obsolete* and *misogynistic* may be included in those comments. *Loony* also.

Mary actually smiles, which makes her glasses slide to the tip of her nose. "If I can just help *one* child."

When John joins us for Tuesday Tea, I decide to test Darcy's story. I pull out a piece of notebook paper.

"Come here, John." I use a velvety voice. "I'd love to have something you wrote in your own hand. I want something to share with my children and grandchildren, so I can say '*the* John Wickham wrote this for me.'" I hand him the paper. I sit down next to him and tuck my hands under my chin. I bat my eyes. "Write a poem for me."

John glows with celebrity. He sits down and writes:

> *Roses are red,*
>
> *Violets are blue,*
>
> *I was told to write this,*
>
> *So that's what I do.*

He signs his name in a weird flourish at the bottom. He is quite pleased with himself.

"Wow. It's puerile," I tell him.

"Thank you," he says.

I am supposed to take the poem as tongue-in-cheek, but I suspect now that it is really the best he can do.

As I stand next to him, I realize the smell of his cologne has changed. It is the same woodsy scent, but my senses take it in differently. There is a strain of decay in it that I had not noticed before. It takes me a moment to identify the stench, but when I figure it out, I can think of it in no other way. It is the awful reek of deception.

"You know," he tells me with his mega-grin, "I've been doing some research. I think I could get you into a house within your budget. It would only take five to six hundred dollars for the paperwork."

I put the poem away. "I'll think about it."

"You do that." Charismatic smile commences.

John moves around The Hemingway Room, talking to all the librarians but Mary. He out-swaggers every man in the room. Eventually, he finds his way to the checkout desk with a book.

I input the information and print out his checkout slip for *Still Stripping After 25 Years*, which he will soon figure out is a how-to about removing wallpaper.

"Thanks for checking me out," he says like a true lothario.

Mrs. Bennet comes straight over. "What a pleasant man he is," she decides as John struts out the door.

After work, I go home and read Darcy's letter once more. The tone, the verbiage, and the fluidity all match those of *Pemberley*.

I do not need to check the real estate listings for John's name. I have no doubt it is not there.

I should not care, but I do. I am now convinced I was wrong about Darcy.

A pirate puppet named Captain Bacon has kidnapped Prince

Porkchop.

"Give me your kingdom, and I will give you back the prince!" the pirate tells Lady Ambrosia. Captain Bacon's thick black eyebrows move up and down with evil intent.

"Oh, no! What shall I do?" Lady Ambrosia asks her audience in high-pitched British helplessness. She clasps her pudgy pig hands together.

The children sitting before the puppet stage are completely entranced by the melodrama. They boo every time the pirate shows his face and clap at the sight of the prince.

For several weeks' episodes, Prince Porkchop pretended to be a common peasant named Louis Hamm. Then, when he had won over the lady's heart, he revealed that he was, in fact, a prince. It is an old story that makes us believe that anything is possible—things can always be better than they appear.

But, what if the opposite were true—a guy pretends to be a prince, then reveals he is a commoner? We would think he is a deceitful, terrible person/pig puppet.

That dumb little Prince Porkchop puppet with only two facial expressions charmed Lady Ambrosia, then gloated in his deception. As though this is a good thing.

I realize I *hate* him. I hate Prince Porkchop. I hate John Wickham.

My rage smolders as Lady Ambrosia uses her wits to foil the pirate and rescue her prince.

"I love you, my prince," the lady declares as she rushes across the stage toward Prince Porkchop.

Boo. Boo. *Boooooo.*

The whole crowd of kids turns around, confused. One girl is clearly perturbed, her hazel eyes shooting daggers in my direction. Even Prince Porkchop drops his jaw.

I guess I said "boo" out loud.

"Uhh. Sorry." And I suddenly have to locate a book on the opposite end of the library.

Time appears to be marching on, and with it is change. Charlotte and Collin's wedding invitation hangs on the library wall. It will be a simple ceremony and modest reception. Of course, Charlotte insists on doing all the prep work herself. Every time I go to her house to see if she needs help, she is up to her elbows in homemade decorations. Although I do not understand her choice, I see her come alive at the prospect of having a family.

"My Collin just signed the papers for a little house next to Mrs. de Bourgh's. It's the surest way to make himself available and prove his loyalty," she tells me. Then she explains each room of her future house in detail, telling me precisely how she will decorate it and make it her own. They plan to have children right away. Charlotte's eyes glow with the endless possibilities. She barely refers to her fiancé in the discussion, only saying something about how it is better to know as little as possible about the "defects" of one's companion prior to matrimony.

"Happiness in marriage is purely a matter of chance," she assures me.

The wait is short. Two weeks later, with Kate de Bourgh's approval, Charlotte and Collin become husband and wife.

Chapter 11

"*Poor Anne*. Her Darcy has gone to Oregon to promote his book." Kate de Bourgh is telling Mrs. Bennet and anyone else who will listen. Anne is standing next to Kate with the same dull expression as always. Mrs. Bennet nods her head in sympathy.

It has been weeks since I have seen Darcy, but the heightened emotions I associate with his name are still too raw. It is a relief he is gone for now.

In quiet moments, I ponder the little reminders of Darcy I see all over the library. Some memories make me wince, remembering my own disagreeable behavior, and others make me smile because I know now that he was thinking of me.

Jane seems so positive outwardly, but I still see signs that she is not the same Jane. There is an extra layer to her guardedness, an extra sting in her usually polite rebuff of male patrons' flirtations. Friendship is a fine balm for disappointed love, but it is not enough. She needs some Charlie.

Lydia, who does not concern herself with our troubles, is giddy with her upcoming birthday. Ever since her grandmother died, she has seen the age of 21 as the year life truly begins. The endless chatter about what she will do with her inheritance fills the down time. *Two hundred grand.* Lydia exclaims, "I'll buy a house. No, I'll buy a nice car and find a rich man to buy me the house."

Calvin Klein bags. Trips to Europe. A major party for all her friends. I do not think Lydia knows there are limits to $200,000, especially after taxes. I mention it, but it does not bother her in the least. She imagines she is like Kate de Bourgh, just without the dead husband.

"How I wish someone would die and leave me two hundred thousand," gripes Kitty. "Or *more*."

"Don't we all?" I chime in.

"Ha, ha," Lydia mocks.

Kitty sulks back to her Korner. And I help Lydia shelve the books.

Lydia has been extra distracted lately—hiding in corners of the library, making secret phone calls and texts. There seems to be an endless pile of returned books she has no desire to deal with. Which means the rest of us must. And without complaint.

Charlotte and Collin occupy a house that seems out of place on Rosings Road—a long, winding street known for its opulence. Their house is an average ranch style home that looks much older than its neighbors. Lining the hilly road are tall, ostentatious houses built for those with wealth to show off.

I knock at the door and Collin and Charlotte spiritedly greet me. Charlotte hugs me and welcomes me inside.

Collin straightaway points out the "marvelous view." Their large picture window in the living room does not showcase a view of the hills or the nearby stream. It frames the home of their neighbors, the de Bourghs. The de Bourgh house is a stunningly conspicuous home, covered in vines and cathedral-like windows. An ugly modern sculpture twists on their front lawn. It is all money and no taste.

Collin insists on taking me on a tour of their home, pointing out the details that Kate de Bourgh assisted them with. He does all the talking while Charlotte stands by.

"This gun rack is *precisely* as she suggested. Rifles spaced just so," he tells me. "Nothing is too small to be beneath Mrs. de Bourgh's notice."

"Ah."

Collin draws a deep breath, then moves on to show me the freezer Kate selected specifically for the size and shape of their home.

"We can fit an entire deer in this freezer," he speculates. "Maybe two."

"Just one," Charlotte corrects.

I picture Collin stomping through the forest, scaring away the deer, fowl, rabbits, and other hunters. It is frightening to think of him with a gun.

Collin suddenly turns to me with a surprisingly sincere look in his eyes.

"I hope, Liz, that you don't think I'm showing this all to you to make you jealous. I realize this would be your life had things between us, you know, worked out."

Food for thought. "I'm not offended by your happiness. The past is the past, I assure you." It sounds diplomatic with a hint of sarcastic.

Collin's cell phone rings. He picks it up with startling alacrity. "Yes. I'm coming. I'm coming!" He dashes out the door toward the "manor."

Charlotte watches her husband go. "He's always running off like that. But, I don't mind having the place to myself."

She sighs and turns to me. "Matrimony seems to suit me, Liz."

I see that it does. "I hope I am as fortunate as you someday."

"I know this isn't what you would have wanted. As for me, I was only dreaming of marriage a couple months ago. Things change so quickly, don't they? You never know what's around the corner."

I do not want *anything* to be around the corner. Not for a long while. My soul could really use a rest.

"We'll see," I say. "Now, *you* show me around the house. There's so much more you could tell me."

God is in the details, they say. Charlotte shares with me the colors she has selected to paint the children's room. She has an afghan nearly finished to match. Everything in her house is neatly organized and clean, the work of hands anxious to be of service.

It is a pleasure to see such nuances through her eyes. I wonder if I ever really understood Charlotte and her need for this type of fulfillment. She does not love her husband, not yet, but what she lacks in love she makes up for in appreciation. Love will come.

As for me, I am determined that only the very deepest love could induce me to matrimony.

It is a lovely night. When I leave Charlotte's house after a delicious homemade dinner, I do not get into my car. I walk. The summer breeze is coming down off the mountains. Everything smells fresh and clean. The sidewalks are softly-lit. It is my much-needed moment of quiet reflection. I wrap my arms around myself, breathe in and out, hoping the acceptance of change is not too far off.

For the most part, the wealthy homes I see around me are a sheer show of vanity. I put my hand on my heart. "My vision is within. *Here* is where the birds sing," I remind myself in E. M. Forster's words. The sentiment is a comfort. It makes me feel less envious, at least.

An image reflecting on a shiny window stops me in my tracks completely. Is that what I think it is?

I swiftly cross the street.

It is *exactly* what I hoped: a large bookshelf. And what a bookshelf! Twelve feet wide, floor to ceiling. Mahogany. It is like a shrine to books. A long ladder rests next to the shelf.

I cannot help it. I abandon the sidewalk and start tip-toeing across the manicured lawn, completely encroaching on the property. I try to stop my feet, but I am like one of those stupid moths drawn to a bluish light that means certain death. Oh, *what* is on that shelf? My imagination knows no bounds. Marilynne Robinson? Peter Taylor? Louise Erdrich? Alice Walker? There has got to be at least one Salman Rushdie or Ellen Glasgow.

I nearly trip on a large landscape rock. I stub my toe on the next one. Sheesh.

I grit my teeth and gawk through the window. Most of the books I can see are of the leather-bound type. They are not just for show, however. The books exhibit definite signs of wear—rough corners and creases in the binding. There are classic authors, such as V.S. Naipaul and Émile Zola, from all over the world. There are biographies, histories, modern classics, how-tos, medical tomes and books of art. Many of the books I have never seen in Longbourn Library. There is even a copy of *Pemberley*.

At the sight of all those books, my spirits soar to a high flutter and something I call the "book shivers" spreads from the top of my head to the bottom of my feet. I have discovered the eighth wonder of the world, right here in Hertford, Idaho.

"What are you doing?" a man's voice asks gruffly.

I freeze.

There is a beam of light in my face. I cannot explain what I am doing here. I am unable to move.

Oh, gosh. I am going to jail.

After what feels like an eternity, the light in my face moves to the ground.

"Good to see you, Liz."

I unfreeze. I recognize that voice. It is much softer than before.

It is Darcy's.

We are inside Darcy's house. I am sitting at the coffee table with the bookshelf towering over me.

I stumble through my words. "I didn't know it was your house. I didn't mean to trespass. I just saw that bookshelf and *all those books*. . ." My arm flails in the direction of the bookshelf.

"You've told me. Six times." He hands me some hot chocolate.

"Just trying to make that clear, you know," I respond mechanically.

I peer out the window into the hills surrounded in darkness, wishing I were lost in the woods being hunted by wolves instead. I would rather be anywhere but here.

This is the most awkward moment of my life. So much for avoiding drama. The hot chocolate shakes in my hands.

Darcy sits down. It is surreal to see him wearing jeans and a T-shirt. Sandals hug his bare feet.

I want to say something, but there seems to be an embargo on every subject. I cannot think of any topic that feels "safe" at this moment. I take a sip of hot chocolate.

Darcy regards me quietly.

Say something, Liz. *Come on.*

"How was your book tour?" I manage to get out. Words feel weird in my mouth. And taste kind of chocolaty.

"I think it went well," he decides. "I read *Pemberley* to more crowds and fielded the same questions in each place. But I hated staying in hotel rooms and meeting so many strangers." He smiles. "I'm glad to be back here."

"Afraid fame would spoil you?"

"According to you, I've already been spoiled too much."

Hmm. I guess I do not like confrontation, either. I drink my hot chocolate in one big, scorching swig.

"Do you know Kate de Bourgh lives just down the street?" I ask.

"I'm fully aware of it. She likes to bring her daughter over once in a while. She thinks we'd be good for each other. I don't see it." He finds an amusing thought. "That hideous sculpture on their lawn gives me nightmares."

"We're in agreement there."

"Your father—is he well?"

I am taken aback. That Darcy can even speak to me at all is amazing—but to speak with such thoughtfulness, to inquire after my family?

"His health is always an issue, but he is in good spirits, thank you."

He nods, but seems concerned.

A *meow*. A white fluffy Persian cat appears. It rubs Darcy's legs and sits in front of me expectantly.

"Who are you, sweetie?" I ask.

"That's William Fitz."

"The author of *Pemberley*? Is that you?"

Meow. He jumps up and sits next to me, purring a loud, rusty purr.

I rub his furry head and he responds with gusto. "Are you writing anything else these days, Mr. Fitz?"

In response, he scratches at his sparkly studded collar.

"I'll answer for him," Darcy says. "He's writing a sequel."

"Is that so? Anything about knickers in it?"

Darcy laughs. "You will never let that go, will you? He might mention them at certain points."

Darcy laughs? Who knew?

"I can't wait to read that. And, thank you, Mr. Fitz. I needed some more fur on these jeans."

It is then I notice the copy of *The Odd Women* sitting on the coffee table. The tattered cover tells me it is an early edition. Instinctively, I reach for it and open it to the front. I gasp. It is a first edition, signed by the author. I run my fingers across George Gissing's scrawl and go numb.

"You have fine taste," I say without thinking.

Suddenly, I realize I just echoed Darcy's words he used when I was reading this book in Longbourn Library.

He was not talking about Lydia's taste in books. He was talking about *mine.*

I look up at Darcy. Our eyes meet. I see the soft, amused look on his face and I stand up so quickly, I hit my knee against the table.

I tell Darcy, "Really, you've been very hospitable, considering the circumstances." I look at the feline. "You too."

"Leaving so soon?"

"I have to work early tomorrow. I don't know what I was

thinking walking around here at this time."

I reach the door. Darcy and the cat are right behind me.

"Ms. Liz?" Darcy's gaze rests on my face. I can barely look at him. "My sister Georgiana is coming to visit soon. Is it all right if I introduce you to her?"

Darcy is like a different person, easy and friendly. He seems so much more relaxed here in his own environment. He is speaking with such gentleness, such thoughtfulness, considering our unexpected meeting tonight. If only I had that level of ease inwardly that he has outwardly right now.

"Yes. I would be delighted to meet her."

There is the smile again. "Thank you. Would you like a ride back to your car?"

"No. I like to walk. Very quickly. I'll be there in no time flat, I'm sure. Thank you again for not calling the police. Umm. Goodbye."

Ugh. I am so inarticulate. Best to leave before it gets worse.

I cannot remember the trip from the house to the car to home. I just realize I am in bed and Mrs. Hill is suspicious of another cat's smell in the air. She rubs my face repeatedly, reclaiming me as her own.

"I'm not going anywhere, sweetie," I assure her.

My mind is not sure of the difference between fiction and what I just witnessed. Did that really happen? Was that *really* Darcy—and was he really wearing *a T-shirt*? What a contrast between the last time I saw him outside Longbourn Library, placing that letter into my hand!

I am not comfortable. It would be impossible to be. I am, however, flattered and pleased Darcy would wish to introduce me, a blatant trespasser, to his sister. I can do nothing but think, and think with wonder, of Darcy's wishing me to meet his sister.

His behavior was so strikingly altered from the man I thought I knew. What can it all mean?

I think I will not sleep. I imagine I will be awake until dawn with so much awkwardness to joggle out of my system. Surprisingly, no. I count the stripes on my wallpaper and fall to sleep quickly. I dream I dance the night away at a ball in an Edith Wharton novel. I wake up fully refreshed.

Chapter 12

John Wickham has shown up a few times at the library now. I have been cold and dismissive with him, firmly saying no to his idea of "investing" in that house. It took a few tries, but he got the hint that all my interest in him and the house has ended. I take comfort that Darcy and John have never crossed paths on Longbourn grounds.

One day, I overhear Lydia grumble, "That nasty, freckled thing. What does John see in *her*?"

I quickly figure out whom Lydia is talking about.

I catch John sitting with Mariah at break time, staring directly into her eyes the way he once gazed into mine. I felt special when he looked at me that way. But I know now it is just him—his signature move. It is a technique he has certainly used dozens of times, even on a naive Georgiana Darcy.

In a spare moment, I corner Mariah to explain how she needs to be careful with the likes of John. She chalks my warning up to jealousy and will not listen.

Within a few days, he dumps her as quickly as he picked her up. John leaves Mariah heartbroken and confused about what she did wrong.

I keep an eye out for him after that, but he seems to have disappeared. Good riddance, John Wickham, you cad.

Darcy sends a card to me, care of Longbourn Library. It is a very formal invitation to his house for dinner.

It is not a date, I tell myself. That chance has passed. I am just meeting his sister Georgiana.

I dress up anyway.

I drive my little truck to the Darcy residence. At the door, I find myself hesitate to knock. It is still incredible to me that Darcy would want me to meet his sister—that he is able to look beyond my unladylike, basically criminal, and horrid behavior.

The door swings open. I'm greeted by a beautiful young girl, around 20, with long dark hair and capped teeth. She has Darcy's dark eyes.

"I thought that might be your truck. I've heard so much about you, Liz," she tells me and pulls me inside.

Darcy appears at her side.

Oh, my gosh. He is wearing an apron. Now *that* is casual. He is the same relaxed, easy-going man I last saw here.

"Ms. Liz, it is an honor to introduce you to my sister, Georgiana."

"A pleasure to meet you, Georgiana," I say, holding out my hand. She ignores the hand and goes in for a hug.

They show me to the living room. The feline Mr. Fitz is sitting on the sofa as if he has been waiting for me.

Darcy backs away. "The food can't cook itself. If you'll forgive me, I'll leave you two—well, *three*—alone."

Georgiana shrugs and smiles. "He cooks. I eat. It's the perfect setup."

We sit down. There is a decidedly lighter feel to this visit than the last one, probably because this time I am *not* committing a crime. Already the smell of steak and potatoes is wafting through the house. I am suddenly hungrier than I thought I was.

I say, "How lucky you are to have a cook. Some of us just order out and microwave." I scratch Mr. Fitz's chin and he seems delighted.

Georgiana says, "Yes, I have the best brother in the world. I've missed him so much since he's been traveling around."

"How long will you be here?"

"Just a couple weeks, until fall semester. I'll take what I can get. And inevitably go back ten pounds heavier, thanks to Will."

"Tell me what you're studying."

"I'm studying ESL. As soon as I graduate, I'm going to head off to Japan or maybe Spain. Wouldn't it be wonderful to live and work overseas?"

"I can think of nothing better. How does your brother feel about your future?"

"Oh, he fully supports me. He helps me study for my exams and he is always sending me links to places abroad that need teachers."

"Have you traveled much?"

Her eyes light up. "*Some.* A trip to Mexico. A semester in Quebec. Just enough to give me a taste for traveling."

Georgiana goes to the large, sublime bookshelf and pulls out an atlas. She guides me through her trips, explaining each place she visited in passionate detail. The way she talks makes it clear she has chosen the best possible major for herself and just looking forward to such journeys is a matter of great importance in her life. Once she completes her tale, she looks up at me. Her very countenance glows with wonderment.

"If adventures do not befall a young lady in her own village, she must seek them abroad," she says. "Isn't that what Jane Austen said?"

I smile. "Word for word. Unfortunately, my adventures have mostly been confined to books. But I would love to see Italy, if I could."

"Like on a honeymoon?"

The question oddly makes my heart hurt. "Any way I can go, I suppose."

Georgiana suddenly gets a faraway look in her eyes. She contemplates something for a moment then looks at me, making her decision to share what she is thinking. "I had my heart broken. *Really* broken," she says.

"I know. I'm sorry."

She searches for the words. "I thought John was so *amazing*, you know, like he was the answer to all my heartache after my parents died. Only—he *added* to it, made it worse. He took my grief to a deeper level."

"It must be hard to trust someone again after that."

"I'm learning. I'm getting there," she says with a reluctant smile. "You know, there are eight billion people in the world. It is crazy, really, to let *one* affect us so much."

"And yet we do."

"That means we are all crazy?"

"If we think we are in love, it often does." I nudge her. "Don't give up. I've heard those Spanish guys are mighty sexy."

Georgiana nods and grins.

Darcy is standing in the doorway. His sister cannot see that he has been listening. His look of concern mixed with protectiveness is unmistakable. He really loves his sister.

"Would you ladies like to come to the dining room?" Darcy asks.

Georgiana looks up. "Absolutely. My new friend is hungry. She told me. Well, her stomach did."

I pat my stomach and respond, "You might say I'm a bit

'peckish.'"

We sit down in the dining room. It is a large, well-proportioned room, handsomely adorned with an ornate Victorian dining table and buffet. I feel dwarfed in my high-back oak chair.

The doorbell rings. Darcy excuses himself.

"Really? Liz is here?" a man's voice says. I recognize it immediately.

Then the man himself appears.

"Charlie!"

"Long time, no see, Liz the librarian. And, Georgiana, of course." He has lost a bit of his tan, but his smile is all there.

I tell Charlie, "How good to see you! I was starting to think you would never come to Hertford again."

"I thought so, too, but then. . . well, I missed this place."

As he slides into the chair next to me, Georgiana excuses herself and joins Darcy in the kitchen.

"Do you like New York?" I ask.

"It is a good place, for one in my line of work. But *this*—this is the place I think of when I think of home. And, out of the blue, Darcy invited me here for a week. I simply could not say no. Now, tell me. How is the library? Tell me everything. How is everyone there? The same librarians are still there, aren't they?"

I am not sure which question to answer. "Yes, we're all still there. Just Lydia will soon leave us."

"Oh, I'm sorry to hear that," he feigns. He gets down to the point. "But, *Jane* is there, right?"

I say it slowly and watch his face, "Jane is still there."

"Oh, I'm so glad." His shoulders drop in relief.

He looks toward the kitchen to see if we are alone, then turns back to me. He whispers, "Is. . .is she seeing anyone?"

I feel the color rise in my face. Charlie is holding his breath, waiting for my answer.

"She's as single as you are, apparently."

He breathes. "Excellent. Truly marvelous. Is the library open now?"

"On a Sunday? No. Now, do you need any books from the library? Something by Dumas, perhaps? I know someone who can give you a good recommendation."

"I will get one. First thing tomorrow morning." His eyes convey every spark of hope in that idea.

Dinner is a lovely and stylish affair. Darcy tosses the apron aside in favor of his black suit. Our meal is delectable steak and potatoes by candlelight.

I forget my formal manners and stuff in several mouthfuls with a shiny silver fork. "My compliments to the chef," I say.

Darcy smiles. "Okay. I'll tell him—Fitzy!" he calls toward the living room.

"Don't *even*. Oh, no. Here he comes."

Meow. The cat jumps onto one of the empty chairs. He sits in a regal manner, as though he knows exactly how much money he cost and feels he is worth every penny. I once again deliver my compliments. "Mr. Fitz, you can cook for me anytime."

He closes his eyes and purrs.

Georgiana tells us about her campus life, classes and activities. She has been dedicating her time to a campus charity project this summer, gathering donations for war-torn parts of the world. I admire her for considering the bigger picture with such passion. She is not one of those out-of-sight-out-of-mind people. Every soul on this earth is a concern to her. Georgiana has my respect.

Georgiana turns to Darcy at one point and starts speaking animated French.

They banter *in French*. I have no idea what they are saying. I feel like I just fell off the turnip truck.

Charlie laughs at the look on my face.

I do not like that. So, I turn to Charlie and start speaking Pig Latin.

"O-day ou-yay eak-spay ig-pay atin-lay?" I ask him.

He catches on, but does not seem to know how to proceed. "Yes-ay?"

"That would be o-nay," laughs Darcy.

Two months ago, I never would have imagined stand-offish Darcy interacting with others this way, least of all me. It is so unexpected. Why is he so altered? It cannot be for my sake that he has softened.

I feel as though I am looking at him through a new lens, one that erases our background differences and prejudgments. I see nothing but an intelligent, handsome, talented man sitting next to me.

Suddenly, however, some unfortunate recollections intrude. I feel that pang of guilt again over how I treated him.

Darcy is watching my face carefully. He stops laughing. "I'm sorry you're uneasy, Liz. Can't we forget the past, just for the evening?"

I agree. I am pleased with his concern, but feel no sense of triumph.

Darcy gently touches my arm, then pulls back.

The touch makes me pleasantly unsteady.

At the sight of Darcy's gesture, a knowing glance passes between Charlie and Georgiana.

Mr. Fitz yawns and bows out of the conversation. He drops down to the floor and heads to a corner to curl up.

Between dinner and dessert, Georgiana shows me an album of family pictures. Her parents are there in the early pictures, absent in the later ones. The father, tall and clean-shaven with the chin of a superhero, looks as though he is ready to lead a meeting of CEOs.

"Our father was an excellent man," Georgiana explains. "He was greatly concerned about the poor and homeless."

Hmm. Is that why generosity seems to run in the family?

Their mother, clearly responsible for her children's dark eyes, has an intense presence. Her clothing too is formal, but her hair and jewelry have an air of "former hippy" to them. I identify something familiar in her face, a connection that goes beyond her resemblance to her children. I tuck the sense of familiarity away and focus on the simple and very real loss of beloved parents.

How much these tragedies can shift the direction of our lives.

Their parents were killed in a car accident four years ago. The trauma of the loss seems to have brought Georgiana and Will Darcy closer as they had to cling to each other through that dark time.

"James and Gina—those are their names, aren't they?" I ask.

Georgiana replies, "Yes. How did you know?"

"Well," I look to Darcy, "*Pemberley* was dedicated to a James and Gina. I only guessed."

Brother and sister look at each other and nod gently.

I pick up a second album marked *Will*.

Darcy's eyes widen. "You can skip that one," he says.

I smile at him and whip the album open. "This is *research*. Trust me, it's all very scientific. Oh, look, even as a baby you wore a suit."

Darcy sits up a little straighter. "My parents had strong ideas about propriety."

"Ah. Now, in this picture, you're wearing your *birthday* suit." There is little baby Darcy, lying on his stomach, grinning at the camera. "Nice cheeks."

Charlie laughs so hard the table shakes.

Darcy clears his throat. "My parents did err from decorum from time to time."

I take my time flipping through picture after picture. Georgiana explains what Darcy stays mum about. There is a six-year-old Darcy in a private school uniform, missing his front teeth. Student of the year. Captain of the ski team. Graduations and awards. He always seemed to be accomplishing something.

A picture of Darcy at the beach. Wet white shirt clinging to his chiseled torso. I linger way too long on that one.

Hot flashes. Pleasantly unsteady again. Okay, album down.

"Dessert?" Darcy asks.

I cannot look at him straight. "Yes, please."

Chocolate mousse never tasted so good. Amongst the four of us there is a great deal of intelligent conversation, complete with touches of literary allusion and quotes of the greats. I feel at home on a level I cannot remember feeling.

I hate to see it end.

Georgiana hugs me fully when I go to leave. Charlie shakes my hand, cheerfully reassuring me he will stop by the library tomorrow.

Darcy, ever formal, walks me to my truck and opens the driver side door for me.

"You were so kind to come. Georgiana really needed that. It's good to see she has found a friend."

"I'm pleased to know her. You demonstrated great discernment when you thought we'd get along."

"I'm not always a good judge of character, but in this case, I was right. I was right about you."

There is something pleasing about Darcy's mouth when he speaks to me, something of dignity that gives me a favorable idea of his heart.

He holds out his hand.

I take it.

His touch is tender and considerate. For a brief second, I feel like a princess in a novel, waiting for the guy on a horse to get down and kiss me already.

"Good night, Ms. Liz."

"Good night, Mr. Darcy."

I long to know what is going through Darcy's mind. Am I still dear to him? There is a possibility that I am. He is becoming dearer to me every moment. But I doubt either of us would be able to put away our pride to admit it.

Chapter 13

Jane looks beguiling when she walks into Longbourn Library Monday morning. That is probably because I called her last night and told her she *needs to look amazing* today. She was suspicious when I would not say why, but she is agreeable enough to put it aside. I was tired of seeing no-makeup-and-dirty-jeans Jane. I have been thinking she is going to show up in sweatpants any day. No more.

The public entrance is still locked. Jane and I are preparing for the small crowd of retired folks that show up to do genealogy at 8:00.

We hear a knock at the window, then see a face. It is Charlie, dressed up and eager. He no doubt is standing in the flower bed. His fingers are wrapped around a bouquet of daisies that I hope did not come from said flower bed.

Jane whispers, "Liz, is it really. . ." But she cannot finish her sentence.

It is ten minutes early, but I get my keys and let Charlie in.

I lead the two lovebirds to The Brink Room, push them in, and close the door.

In the afternoon, I hear the distinct sound of sobbing coming from the restroom. I peer inside.

Jane's face is red and streaked, but she is smiling.

She manages, "Charlie couldn't wait to take me to dinner, so he brought me lunch. It was our first date. We sat on that bench outside and he told me. . .he told me he missed me every day he was gone." Nose blow; sniff. "I thought he had forgotten me—and why wouldn't he? We never had any kind of *understanding*, to use an old word for the matter. You *know* I couldn't forget him. I imagined he'd found some New York 'socialite.' I was *so sure* of it. I had to just pray he was content. That had to be enough. I didn't think I could let myself hope." More tears form and start down her cheeks. "I didn't know—I just couldn't imagine I would be this happy, Liz."

I grab another tissue for her. "You don't *look* happy, Jane. And your makeup is going everywhere. I've never seen you so discomposed."

She smiles through the tears and sniffs hard. "Then I hope I'm never composed again. I'm truly lucky, aren't I?"

"That's not luck. It is everything you deserve."

She dabs at her eyes. "Charlie's moving here to Hertford. He called his boss and quit while I was sitting there."

"He doesn't waste much time, does he?"

She shakes her head no.

Jane does not have to tell me. It is there to be seen. She loves him already and I have no doubt the reverse is the same.

She says, "Oh, no. Help me clean up my face. He's taking me to dinner as soon as I get off work."

"So soon? You already had lunch together."

She shrugs and grins. "He can't wait."

It is all too much for Mrs. Bennet. She spotted Jane and Charlie eating lunch and immediately came over to Longbourn Library. She does not rest until she has squeezed every librarian and patron for an ounce of gossip. Mrs. Bennet's voice carries too loudly, in non-stop tittering, throughout the building.

Mrs. Bennet ambushes Jane as soon as she exits the bathroom.

"Well, Jane. Charlie has come back, has he? I was sure we'd never see him again for a while there, but I am happy to be wrong on that point. He is very welcome to come back to Hertford, however. Who knows what may happen now."

Jane blushes at that last statement.

Mr. Bennet, who has been trying desperately to read in peace, offers Jane congratulations, checks out *No Country for Old Men*, then announces he is going home.

As he shuffles out, it vexes me no end how he married such a woman as Mrs. Bennet. Happiness in marriage cannot be entirely a matter of chance.

There is an unusually large stack of books waiting to be shelved. I scan the room for Lydia, but she is not there. I realize I have not seen her all day and the drama with Jane and Charlie had put her out of my mind.

A feeling of dread comes over me. Did Lydia take the bookmobile out for a joyride again?

I ask Kitty if Lydia is sick.

Kitty looks as though she has just been caught with her hand in the cookie jar. "No. She quit."

"Already? I thought she had two days left."

"Yes, but something came up." Kitty is not looking me straight in the eyes.

I begin sorting and alphabetizing the stack of books. There is no one else to do it. The checkout line is short enough Jane can manage.

A hard push gets the book cart moving. I maneuver the squeaky contraption to the nearest shelf. The first book in hand, *Things Fall*

Apart, slides nicely into the gap left by the Achebe novel. I grab the next in the stack.

Lydia did not say goodbye. That is hardly like her. She never passes up a chance to be the center of attention. She was always talking about how we would have to buy her flowers and gifts when she left. She was not kidding.

Something just does not feel right.

Next thing I know, it is nearly closing time. The patrons have been asked to leave so we can lock up. Kitty is in her Korner, setting up the puppet show for tomorrow morning. I walk past her desk and the cell phone sitting there buzzes and lights up.

"We R nearly there! Reno here we come!" a message shouts. It is from Lydia.

"Kitty—Lydia's going to Reno?" I ask.

Kitty lays Lady Ambrosia down. The lady pig flops against the table and looks at me.

"Yes," Kitty says quietly.

"*That's* why she couldn't come to work today? What about her party? She said for sure she'd stay a couple more days."

"It's for. . .a job." Kitty says it more like a question, as though wondering if I will believe it.

"A job? *Why*? What's going on?"

Jane and Mary stop what they are doing and step closer to listen.

Kitty says, "She's going to be a model."

Jane, Mary, and I look at each other and we tacitly agree Lydia is delusional. Kitty possibly as well.

I conclude, "Lydia's five foot four and 150 pounds. She's not going to be a model, least of all in a place like Reno."

"Her boyfriend is an agent. He said she's beautiful and she'll definitely make some good money in the Reno market."

Mary crosses her arms, hating the idea that any kind of "sin city" exists in the world, no doubt.

Jane and I share a terrified look.

"*Boyfriend?*" we ask at the same time. Lydia has never failed to tell us all about her boyfriends in the past.

My stomach churns.

There is no way around the next question. "Dare I ask who her boyfriend-slash-agent is?" I ask, already knowing the answer.

Kitty sheepishly pulls a fashion magazine out of her drawer. Scrawled on the front, in familiar handwriting, is a phone number and the name *John Wickham*.

Jane, Mary, and I all try calling Lydia. We dial John's number he left on the magazine. They both block us. I am sure John has convinced Lydia we are trying to sabotage her career. There is no doubt he has got his eye on her bank account that will grow exponentially in the next few days. Why not run up some Reno fun and charge it to Lydia? He will have her paying him cash for photo shoots and advertising she will never see. He will promise her work that never materializes while they blow through her two hundred grand. I feel *sick*.

I should have seen it coming. The drama of late clouded out all the signs. Lydia, who could not keep her mouth shut about her inheritance, opened herself up to all kinds of gold-digging. And there was John, opportunist and con artist, ready to make his move. I think of all the curious, secretive texting Lydia has been doing lately. She was texting *him*.

What can I do? Drive to Reno and search the whole city?

We call Lydia's father and break the news. He says he will get on an airplane as soon as possible.

Mary reminds us all, "We cannot be too guarded towards undeserving men." Then she leaves, shaking her head. The situation is something so far out of her comfort zone, it is best to let others take care of it.

"Jane, we can't do anything else. Go to dinner with Charlie."

She is sitting with her head in her hands. "You warned me, Liz. You told me there was something deceitful about John."

"And you thought the best of him. There's nothing wrong with that. I love that you don't take much stock in gossip. I am the one who's known his true character without a doubt and never told anyone most vulnerable to his predatory skills. Lydia is the first person I should have told. I should have told you, too, Kitty."

Kitty breaks into tears. Her curls fall forward and stick to her cheeks.

"There is nothing more we can do, ladies. Let's go," I say.

Jane and Kitty take a reluctant exit. I lock up.

I scan the near-empty parking lot and the sky, wondering what more I can do to disable this feeling of helplessness.

Lydia, you foolish girl. *What* have you done?

"I thought the library closed later. At least I get to see you." It is Darcy's voice. He is dressed up, smells divine. His face is open and lovely.

If only I could see him alone under different circumstances.

"We close at six in the summer. Lydia ran off with John Wickham." I say it all in one breath.

His smile instantly vanishes. "Say that again?"

I tell Darcy the whole story—every detail I know. He becomes visibly upset, pacing back and forth. I have ruined his night, I am sure.

"This is my fault," he tells me. His voice conveys my own fears. He has lost all his ease.

"No, this is my fault. I *knew* what John was. I should have warned everyone at the library, everyone in the *world*, about him."

Darcy turns to me, distress worrying his face. "Please don't think that way. I could have turned John into the police years ago with what I know about him. If my father hadn't thought so well of him, I would have."

"I hope Lydia's father can locate them, maybe by searching hotels. Should I call the police?"

He shakes his head. "She hasn't been kidnapped. We know she went freely. There are lots of "agents" out there with less of a résumé than John. No, the police won't do anything about Lydia, especially across state lines."

I feel more powerless than before. And now I have troubled Darcy.

The determination in his manner ignites, then explodes.

"I have to leave," he declares.

I would not think to stop him. Instinctively, I hold out my hand. Darcy grabs it and shakes it in a hard, businesslike manner. "Goodbye, Ms. Liz."

I step back, a bit stunned by his brusk manner. "Bye, Darcy."

In three seconds, he is in his Volvo. The car makes an imprudent squeal and hastens out of the Longbourn Library parking lot.

The sudden quiet is jarring.

Chapter 14

"I'm glad I never had such a nonsensical daughter. You've done me proud, Lizzie."

It is particularly refreshing to see my father's face—everything from his gap-toothed smile to the bushy eyebrows. His donkey laugh is soothing and *real* in a way that reaches the deepest turmoil in my soul.

I drove the few hours to Boise on Friday night and by Sunday night, I decided to use up some vacation time for Monday and Tuesday. I just could not be in Hertford with that cloud of guilt and anticipation hanging over me. A visit to my father was long overdue, anyway.

My father entertains me with stories of the other residents who all call him Stumpy. They like to tease him to the point he takes off his fake leg and throws it across the room at them.

So much of his seriousness has faded with time. He is not the bitter, nightmare-riddled man I struggled to understand as a child. Whatever demons he grappled with no longer harm him. Even in his confined room, knowing his future certainly involves a gradual decline and inevitable end, he finds joy in the simple things. Like a visit from his only child.

We reminisce. We talk about the latest books we have read. He points out the nurse he has a crush on. Visiting hours pass rapidly every day.

Every evening, I call Jane. No news. Just the frantic weight of misinformation and lack of leads. Desperation agitates my nerves, though I do not make the show of it Mrs. Bennet would. To rattle myself further, I have a dream in which I see Lydia holding all that cash and dimply John is happily slipping $100 bill after $100 bill from her grasp.

A girl whose nonsense has run unchecked her whole life and a man whose scheming knows no bounds equal a train wreck—a *preventable* train wreck. If I had just gotten my head out of the clouds for a few moments, *really* thought about other people, I would have spotted this peripheral disaster-in-the-making. I should have said something about John. This worrisome situation batters my mind.

But my father brings me back to center with patience and insight. He jokes. He takes this *mountain* that looms so large in my mind and reduces it to the molehill it really is. "The world has not ended, it just feels like it has," he reminds me. "This too will pass."

He is right. I just need to breathe and let this pass.

I cannot imagine the hole that my father would leave if he one day simply *left*. Like the parents of Georgiana and Will Darcy.

Darcy.

"Remember once I told you I'd met a single guy, but I thought he was a snob?" I ask my dad.

"I recall that, yes."

"I was. . ." The words are hard to find. "I was quick to judge him. Too quick."

"*Ah.* Get it out."

I do not have to wait for his questions and he does not interrupt me at all. I tell him everything I can about Darcy from my first impressions to my sharp rejection to dinner at his home. Even the trespassing and the wet white shirt find their way into the story. All the while, my father is scratching his chin, attentively grunting approval or disapproval. He nods appreciatively when I tell him Darcy wrote

Pemberley. By the time I get to the end of my tale, I am flustered and embarrassed. Quite exhausted.

"Where is this guy now?"

"He's gone. He heard about Lydia and John and got away from me as fast as he could."

"What's his name again?"

"Not that it matters, but it's Darcy."

"Peculiar name for a man."

"Well, he *is* from *California*."

My father's equine laugh takes over his whole body. And I laugh, too, until my side aches, because life is funny business. I long for the day I do not take it all so seriously.

Once I get back to my motel, I check my phone. Jane tried to call twice, but I had accidentally turned the sound off.

Before I can call back, my phone rings. It is Jane again. I cannot pick it up fast enough.

"Lydia's back. John is in jail," she says, breathless.

"Oh, my gosh." The relief is palpable. "And, her money?"

"She has every penny."

All the anguish I have been feeling vanishes in that instant. I collapse onto the bed. "You're kidding! That's far better than any of us could have hoped."

"It *is* amazing. Everyone is just *pleased*. Everyone but Lydia, of course."

"I *always* distrusted John Wickham," I hear Mrs. Bennet say. Her shrill voice carries so well.

A mumble in the background disrupts Mrs. Bennet and Jane

replies "What?" away from the phone. She listens a moment, then continues, "Oh, okay. Mary wants me to tell you that she has come to understand that we all have trials in life, but they often lead to something good."

"Thank her for her insight. But, what is John in jail for?"

"Fake IDs. Someone tipped off the police."

"That rotten piece of horse muffin." My temperature spikes. All my anxiety rushes back and I fight for air. I inhale several times. Jane patiently waits. I call John several more fairly innocuous names and I am almost back to normal. "Okay, John has got his comeuppance. Let's focus on the positive. Thank you, dear friend. Thank you for the good news."

"Night, Liz."

"Night."

On the drive home to Hertford, my mind slips back to a moment when I was at Darcy's house for dinner. I took a restroom break, but got lost in the large maze of his house. Rather than open a restroom door, I opened one leading to Darcy's study. The smell of Darcy's cologne filled the space that held a Cherrywood desk topped with stacks of papers, notebooks, and books marked with sticky-tabs. I imagined the open laptop was waiting for Darcy's gentle touch to input the perfect words to complete his next novel. I suddenly felt I was on sacred ground and tiptoed back out, fighting the urge to sneak a peek at his next bestseller in whatever form it may be in.

My whole life, up until that moment, I naively believed all my most beloved books emerged from the ether in their perfect form. I did not consider that behind every piece of true book magic was the only person who could perform such tricks: a magician such as Darcy.

The instant Lydia returns to Hertford, her father makes her put her money into some kind of security account so she does not have access to much of it at one time. This, to some extent, should keep her money less vulnerable. She seems oblivious that such a life-altering calamity was averted.

"You should all go to Reno," Lydia tells us just after we open the library.

She no longer works here, but she manages to come on time for once. She is wearing new clothes, an expensive watch.

With a loud sigh, Lydia tosses her Prada bag onto the counter for all of us to see, then announces, "I never realized how absolutely *dull* Hertford is. We don't have huge magic shows and slot machines and buildings over two stories high."

Mary retorts, "The pleasures of Reno would have no charms for me. I would infinitely prefer a book."

"That explains a lot about you, Mary," snorts Lydia. "For the rest of you, I'll take all of you there. John knows lots of people in Reno. I'll find you all boyfriends."

Kitty is nodding her head.

"No. I don't like your way of getting boyfriends, Lydia," I tell her. "Neither does Kitty."

Kitty is not buying it, but she half agrees.

"I have a boyfriend," Jane beams. She loves to mention Charlie.

Mary, who has been crossing her arms this whole conversation, says, "I can't trust your judgment, Lydia. Your 'boyfriend' is in jail."

"My John is *innocent*. He told me it was all a misunderstanding.

He just needs a bunch of bail money and he will be out soon," Lydia says with a surly face, "but my *father* made sure I can't help him out."

Now she is angry. "Oh, I should have *married* John when he suggested it. The chapel was right there. But I knew I needed the right dress and Kitty for a bridesmaid. . ."

Kitty slides her hands across her clothes as though imagining the bridesmaid dress.

Lydia goes back to surly. "Then the *police* showed up."

Jane and I look at each other and shake our heads in subtle agreement that the situation was worse than we thought. John had Lydia duped on a number of levels, going for whichever one was working. I am disgusted—almost physically ill. Jane, Mary, and I suddenly need to get back to work.

I start prepping The Hemingway Room for our Tuesday Tea. Lydia follows me, still needing an audience. I begin to set up the folding chairs as she plays with the stack of napkins on the table.

"You know," she tells me, "a rather small investment in a blackjack game can give you an amazing return."

I flinch at the word "investment."

Lydia continues, "John promised me he could double my money, so I lent him some. Just $10,000 to start."

I cannot believe I am hearing this.

She keeps going, "But luck wasn't on his side. It just wasn't his day." Her tone is so careless. "So, I lent him more because his luck had to turn at some point, didn't it? In the end, he lost $50,000, but the casino gave it all back."

Hold on. "The *casino* gave it back?" I pull another chair off the rack.

"Yes, after Darcy explained everything to them. They were very nice about it."

Wait—*what?* "You saw *Darcy* there?" I lose my grip and the chair crashes to the floor.

Lydia's hands fly up to her mouth and the napkins tip into a messy pile on the table. "Oh, *no*. I said it. He made me promise, too. No one is supposed to know he was there. You won't say a word, will you?"

"*Why* was he there? *How* did you see him?"

"Oh, he just happened to be at the same hotel. When he ran into us at the blackjack table, he asked us how much money we were down. So, I told him."

Lydia's face goes sullen again. "That's when the *police* showed up and took John away. I don't know how they knew where he was."

I do.

I have to ask, "Now *how* did you get your money back?"

"Oh, simple. Darcy knows the manager at the casino. He told me he'd go talk to him and next thing I know, Darcy brings all my money back. My father showed up soon after."

I have to sit down.

$50,000. Darcy gave her *$50,000*. This clueless, petty little girl.

Lydia is already heading out of The Hemingway Room. She suddenly stops in the doorway, turns on her heels and reminds me, "*Don't* tell about Darcy."

Then she flits away.

I nod, too stupefied to speak.

It is my turn to read for Tuesday Tea this afternoon. Usually, I am excited about the chance to locate a piece of beautiful, possibly obscure, poetry and take a moment to share it publicly. I love the appreciation, adore how the patrons close their eyes when a poem particularly speaks to them.

However, at this moment, I feel empty, almost frozen inside. I wonder if stealing another person's words is the only way I can speak at all.

I choose to read "Her Vesper Song" by Madison Cawein. I stand up, barely able to will my legs to move properly. My whole soul is somewhere else, shaken by the emotional earthquake that ripped through me earlier.

My voice wavers. I begin:

> *The summer lightning comes and goes*
> *In one pale cloud above the hill,*
> *As if within its soft repose*
> *A burning heart were never still -*
> *As in my bosom pulses beat*
> *Before the coming of his feet.*

I focus on each word as it comes before me. I struggle to steady my voice and do justice to the lovely poetry I am highlighting. It takes every ounce of my strength.

> *All drugged with odorous sleep, the rose*
> *Breathes dewy balm about the place,*
> *As if the dreams the garden knows*
> *Took immaterial form and face -*
> *As in my heart sweet thoughts arise*
> *Beneath the ardour of his eyes.*

I look up. Instantly, a deep breath of healing moves through me.

Darcy is *there*, at the back of the room, his eyes fixed on me.

At the sight of his merciful smile, my soul unburdens itself as though I simply shrugged my shoulders and the weight of the world dropped off.

I blink a few times. I find my courage.

I continue:

> *The moon above the darkness shows*
> *An orb of silvery snow and fire,*
> *As if the night would now disclose*
> *To heav'n her one divine desire -*
> *As in the rapture of his kiss*
> *All of my soul is drawn to his.*

This time, I close my eyes for a moment, savoring the words a long-dead poet wrote just for me.

Now to conclude:

> *The cloud, it knows not that it glows;*
> *The rose knows nothing of its scent;*
> *Nor knows the moon that it bestows*
> *Light on our earth and firmament –*
> *So is the soul unconscious of*
> *The beauties it reveals through love.*

I finish that last word slowly, truly considering its depth and forms for the first time. I recognize a spark inside me, a possibility that flows toward me directly from the man in the black suit.

Darcy. I have to tell him *thank you, thank you, thank you.* He needs to know how idiotic I was for turning him down. A million thoughts cloud my mind.

Unfortunately, Mrs. Bennet gets to him before I can. She

launches into the story of Lydia's scandalous trip to Reno—everything he already knows, but cannot let on about. He is polite, humoring her, but steals an occasional glance my direction. He does not smile or encourage Mrs. Bennet to say more. Yet, she prattles on.

I stand a few feet away, anxiously awaiting a moment I can cut in.

After a barrage of details and insinuations, Mrs. Bennet finally completes her tale. She concludes with, "And, you, Mr. Darcy—or, Mr. Fitz, if you prefer—how is your book promotion going?"

He answers her by looking at me. There is such a tender intensity in his eyes. "I have several upcoming readings. In fact, I'm going back to California tonight. I'm just here to say goodbye."

I feel a crack start in my heart. I say, "You're leaving? So *soon*?"

"I have some readings and signings scheduled out there. I also need to take Georgiana home. Really, I didn't mean to stay here as long as I have."

"Well, I'm glad you did. For what it's worth," I tell him, once again struggling to control my voice.

"Me too."

"Oh, *Anne* will miss you so much, Darcy." Mrs. Bennet throws me a "hands off" look.

What can I say at this delicate moment? "You know, Idaho is an easy distance away from California, from what I hear."

He looks me straight in the eye. "It is."

There is a short distance between the two of us at the moment, but I have never felt so far away from someone. I want to run straight into his arms and beg him to stay. I hold back, offering him my hand instead. "Good luck."

Darcy does not seem to know how to respond. He gives a soft "thank you," then his warm hand gently takes mine. We touch a little too long. The crack in my heart spreads.

"Goodbye, Ms. Liz."

Oh, how did we reach the goodbyes so quickly? I cannot process it all so fast. I somehow respond, "Goodbye, Mr. Darcy."

Did he hear my heart completely shatter in the middle of that phrase? He opens his mouth as though wanting to say something more, then closes it again. He is still looking at me, not ready to part, either.

Mrs. Bennet jumps in. "Oh, goodbye, dear Darcy. You'll come again soon, I hope. Don't leave *Anne* waiting too long."

"Liz," Mariah startles me. "I can't get the CD player to work."

"Oh, okay," I say as Mrs. Phillips steps in to monopolize Darcy's attention.

I go to the opposite side of the room and look the CD player over. As I try to figure out if the cord is plugged in properly, my mind is racing. I cannot let Darcy just leave this way. I need to get him alone, tell him I know about his helping Lydia.

It takes a minute, but I realize the cord comes from some other electric device. I locate the correct cord, plug it in, and push "play." Mariah's selection of brass band music thumps out of the player. Now I just need to wait for my chance to get Darcy alone.

I spot Mrs. Phillips, now in deep gossip mode with Mrs. Bennet.

I look about the room at each face and instantly realize one unbearable fact: Darcy is gone.

Chapter 15

"No way."

Comb-over guy's face is a study in incredulity. He stands before the checkout desk scratching at his balding pate.

I explain, "It is a fact. *The Darwin Awards 4* was due months ago. You owe $6.00 for that book alone." This book is a collection of true stories of people who volunteered, so to speak, to exit this world by doing brainless things that ended their lives.

"Uh. My brother borrowed my library card."

Not again. Oh, where is Jane when you need her?

A guy with a mullet and backward baseball cap steps over. The resemblance between the men is startling. "What'd I do this time?"

Comb-over guy gives him a look of hopeful complicity. "You borrowed my library card." He nudges him.

Mullet guy's face transforms into its own peculiar type of disbelief. He turns to me and leans against the counter. "Naw. Don't listen to Brett. I didn't even know where the library was until today." He gives me a toothy grin. "Is his book late again?"

"Yep. He needs to return *The Darwin Awards 4*."

The brother nearly slides off the counter as he breaks into a wobbly laugh and slaps Brett on the arm. "Remember that story about them. . ." He starts laughing so hard he cannot talk. After a solid thirty seconds, he wheezes deeply and grabs his brother's shoulder to steady himself. "Remember that guy that tried to drive his motorcycle with his feet and died cuz of his own flippin' stupidness?"

"Course I remember! I read that story to ya, Bill!"

Bill turns to me with a look of familiarity, as though we have been conspiring against Brett from the beginning. "What Brett don't know is I dropped that book in the toilet." He makes a whistling sound and hand motion of the book heading downward, followed by a "splash" with upturned fingers. "Had to throw it out on account of where it had been and what it had been floating next to."

"*That's* where it is! You owe this lady *six bucks*."

"You borrowed the book!"

"You dropped it in the flippin' toilet!"

They are ready to start punching each other.

I referee, "*Gentlemen*. How much change do you have between you? Do me a favor here."

They put down their fists and dig into their pockets. Soon a pile of small coins and pocket lint yields enough to cover the cost of the charge. Brett's pile of coins reeks of engine oil; Bill's smells like beer. I get a tissue and scrape the change off the counter and into the cash box. "Thank you, boys."

The two brothers walk out, still arguing about who owes whom how much. I try to memorize their names so I will recognize them in *The Darwin Awards 5*.

In that little slice of time, I long for grace and intelligence. I have never thought of myself as a snob, but perhaps I am.

My mind is where my heart is. It is with Darcy.

California. Who would have thought that place I briefly visited so many years ago would have such a strong connection to me now?

I close my eyes and gather up the details of my trip as though they are scraps of paper scattered on the floor. First, a street covered in sidewalk stars, perfect for my impromptu variation of hopscotch. Hands in the pavement; my father appreciating some left by a woman named Marilyn. Then a venture into the wondrous Disneyland. Pictures with princesses. A ride where I was splashed with gallons of water as I clung to my father. After that, a long winding drive through the mountains to see an enormous tree funnily named General Sherman. Finally, Sacramento, what my father referred to as the "heart of California," where the state capital building dwarfed me with its Neoclassical façade.

To pass the time between destinations, my father and I played a game, giving ourselves points every time we saw a business sign, street sign, or other public reference to citrus fruit. I racked up hundreds of points, easily beating my father, who, in hindsight, likely let me win.

A final detail comes to mind: a large truck full of oranges. We followed it along the freeway for miles. As I watched the mammoth mound of oranges jiggle with the movement of the truck, a single orange came loose and bounced down the mound, then onto the freeway in front of our car. Forevermore I would associate that singular, bouncy fruit with the state of California.

I get a friend request on my social media site. It is from Georgiana.

I found you! she writes.

I immediately accept. We message back and forth about her life and she tells me how excited she is that Darcy is closer by. I want to ask about him, but I cannot bring myself to do it. Georgiana and I chat about books, movies, clothes. We delve into that realm of the pain of losing a parent—or two, in her case. She credits her brother for getting her through and keeping her going.

Me: *An ideal older brother?*

Georgiana: *I could not ask for a better or a kinder one.*

Me: *This isn't really Darcy, is it?*

Georgiana: *No. It's Georgiana. Hahahaha.*

It is a full hour of reconnecting and learning more about each other. It is funny, but it feels as though Georgiana and I have known each other years, not weeks. I take note of the connection and credit Darcy for seeing that his sister and I would be "kindred spirits."

Georgiana: *It's late. But I have one more question for you.*

Me: *Shoot.*

Georgiana: *Did my brother ever ask you out? I asked him about that once, but he changed the subject.*

The answer is very simple.

Me: *He did.*

Georgiana: *Then you must have turned him down.*

Me: *Yes.*

Georgiana: *Can you tell me why?*

My fingers pause on the keyboard. The Charlie story is not mine to tell. And, I cannot mention John to Georgiana without causing her a lot of pain.

Me: *Let's just say it was a big misunderstanding.*

Georgiana: *Okay. I'll take what I can get. Thank you.*

Me: *Good night.*

Georgiana: *Good night, dear friend.*

Absence makes the heart grow fonder, but when you mix that

extra fondness with the feeling of being abandoned, you feel nothing but discord for days on end. Darcy's absence is my steady torment. The library feels callous and empty.

I help the new librarian put away some books and I come across *A History of Britain*, a book Darcy once checked out. Just holding the book triggers something in me. A desperation rises. The whole world feels irrational and unfair. What can I do? I need Darcy's warm hand around mine or nothing will ever feel right again.

I find myself seeking out romance novels—the kind where you *know* the two main characters will be getting together. I skip the *Anna Karenina*s altogether and go for the "happy" love stories. Only, I cannot finish them. I always read them until the main characters are on the verge of declaring their love. And I stop. I put the books down as though there is still a chance somehow the characters will not make the right choice, they will not get together. That little sliver of a chance holds me back every time.

"I was so wrong about Darcy," I tell Jane when we are alone.

Jane lifts an eyebrow. "I was wondering when you'd fully admit it."

I swing my chair toward her. "How could I have been so blind, Jane? He was right there in front of me the whole time and I couldn't see him."

"You judged him. We all did. That suit he wears. . ."

I laugh until it hurts. "I *love* Darcy's suit. I love his sideburns. I love his taste in books."

"Tell me truthfully, Liz. How long have you felt this way about Darcy?"

I cannot fix my mind on the moment it started. I was in the

middle before I knew it had begun. "It's been coming on so gradually. But if I search my memory, it could well be the moment I saw his bookshelf."

"Liz! You are so funny."

"I can't help it. It's *huge*."

It is easier to joke than to face myself, of course. In reality, I feel such contempt for myself at moments, I wonder how Darcy can feel anything else toward me. And yet, his willingness to overlook my mistakes proves he is far more of a gentleman than I ever would have guessed when I first met him. His care for his sister demonstrates a rare level of loyalty. His behind-the-scenes rescue of Lydia, too, shows me he operates selflessly, courageously. Darcy could well be the best man I have ever met.

I am not in a state of bliss. There is no euphoria to elevate me. I am pragmatic and trusting, resolved to be the best person I can be, if only for the sake of Darcy's memory. I rejected him in a horribly cruel fashion and no matter what I feel now, I cannot change that.

Another chuckle rumbles across the room. Then a snicker. And a full-bellied chortle, followed by a snort. Mr. Bennet is having a party of one today, curled up in his striped chair.

When he laughs, I laugh also. I cannot help it.

Jane too has full red cheeks, proof of her suppressed giggles.

Serves us right.

Mr. Bennet trudged in this morning, getting an earful of Mrs. Bennet's latest gossip. He walked past the checkout desk and gave me that "help me" look.

Mr. Bennet does not live a life of high drama, but listens to the smallest details of others' lives turned into an over-the-top, fantastical, and exhaustive story *every flipping day*. If anyone needs a touch of healing levity, it is he. Luckily, a library bears similar qualities to a hospital. Librarians are like doctors, books the prescriptions.

I headed to the G's, pulled out *Cold Comfort Farm*, and placed it in Mr. Bennet's hands. If any book can poke fun at melodrama better, I would be hard pressed to find it.

Mr. Bennet turned the Stella Gibbons classic over for the description, then gave me an agreeable nod. It has been years since I read that book, but once Mr. Bennet began, I started recalling every silly moment in turn as though I were reading it along with him. And so did Jane.

The florid, British language of *Cold Comfort* juxtaposed with the sheer hilarity of the parody tickles the senses. I knew Mr. Bennet would take a liking to Mr. Mybug and his obsession with. . .uh, *nature*. Every time I imagine Aunt Ada Doom mentioning how she "saw something nasty in the woodshed," I nearly fall off my chair.

Two pages in, the contagious laughter began. Two hours later, it is still going.

Mary gives us her *shhhhh* glare, but that only makes us howl.

A patron hesitates to approach the checkout as though there may be an outbreak of lunacy starting here in Longbourn Library. I check out her books quickly, and she exits the building as fast as possible.

Another guffaw from the striped chair.

"Mr. Bennet is starting to wear on my nerves a bit," Mrs. Bennet lets us know in a loud whisper.

Ouch. My side hurts and my eyes are watering.

Wow. I needed this.

I needed this too.

Charlie has found a local job for now. It is enough to keep him near Jane.

"Oh, Liz. I was so nervous to meet his parents last week," Jane tells me when I visit at her apartment. "I was so scared they wouldn't like me. I am sorry to be ungenerous, but they seemed so *disapproving* and inconvenienced by the trip out here. They really looked down on me. Charlie, however, would not let them utter *one word* against me. He talked endlessly about the things he likes about me—some things I didn't even realize. It was almost embarrassing how he went on and on about my 'beautiful heart.' He says I have impeccable taste in books, clothes, art, jokes, political parties, toothpaste. . ."

I laugh at that one.

"*Seriously*, Liz! And he has never disliked one of my recommendations. If that is not a compliment, I don't know what is. Did you know he noticed how I always turn pages with my thumb instead of my index finger? *I* was barely aware I do that. Not that it's a virtue, or anything, but he sure makes it sound like it is. Charlie notices things. He makes me feel *appreciated*."

"He's one of the good ones," I say, trying to get a word in edgewise.

"Exactly. Charlie is everything a man should be: sensible, good-humored, lively, and well-mannered. He's everything I ever wanted. To make a long story short, his parents came around. Said they approved."

"Of *course* they did," I say. I am insanely happy for Jane and not the least bit surprised at the result.

A knock sounds at the door.

"That would be Charlie with dinner."

Jane hops up and opens the front door. From the multiple takeout bags on Charlie's arms, I surmise we will be having Mandarin House, KFC, and Taco Time. Jane takes a bag or two from him.

Charlie nods toward me, then informs Jane, "I wasn't sure what your guest would like, so I got a bit of everything."

"That's quite thoughtful of you, Charlie," she tells him, carrying what she can into the kitchen.

"Not at all. And, how are you, Liz?"

"Doing well. Jane was just telling me how the visit from your parents went."

He lights up. "Ah, yes. It went splendidly. How could anyone not love Jane?"

"Indeed."

At the sound of the rustling plastic bags, Guinevere, Jane's old cat, looks up from her spot on the couch and lets out a scratchy meow.

Charlie assures her he also got dinner for her, and the lady kitty yawns and drops off the couch in a lazy thump. We watch the cat waddle into the kitchen.

"Poor old thing," I say. "I understand, Charlie, you have a feline visitor right now. How is Mr. Fitz doing these days?"

Charlie considers. "He's healthy, happy. But, to be honest, he misses you."

"He really does," Jane says from the other room.

I gather my thoughts, considering the information from a different angle. Are we talking about the cat? If not, there is only one thing I could convey about the matter. "Then the feeling is mutual."

Charlie looks at me a moment, a touching look of empathy on

his face. "Dinner?" he asks, cheerful as ever.

Dinner is obviously an eclectic mix of whatever the restaurants on Yellowstone Avenue were offering. I end up with a burrito, a chicken leg, egg-drop soup, and a fortune cookie that tells me "It is up to you to create the dream you long for."

Jane, if she notices the burned nature of her egg rolls, does not let on. It is the good company that takes precedence, and no one minds.

Guinevere gnaws toothlessly on some pieces of chicken in the corner.

Jane and I listen to Charlie's New York stories—tales of subways and Central Park; tales of longing for Jane as he was standing on streets surrounded by skyscrapers.

"My mind said I belonged there," he explains. He takes Jane's hand. "But my heart just couldn't agree."

Jane, possibly more smitten than ever, kisses his hand. "I still can't believe you thought me indifferent."

Charlie takes on a look of seriousness, of contrition. "Mistakes were made," he says, as though directing it at both of us, "with the best of intentions. But that is all in the past. All is forgiven."

The air is heavy for a moment, each of us thinking of the assumptions that nearly ended this romance. I search my heart and find I cannot blame anyone for it: not Charlie, not Jane.

Not Darcy.

"Balderdash," says Jane in her sweet tone.

"What?" Charlie says, alarmed.

"Anyone up for a game of *Balderdash*?"

Charlie's worry transforms into a smile. He slaps the table. "I'd love one! You, Liz?"

"Absolutely."

The game is diverting to say the least. Making up alternative meanings for obscure words, we all laugh through the silliness.

Guinevere joins us and meows out her answers. I have to give her a playing piece to bat around on the floor so she will stop knocking ours off the table. In the end, I feel bad about beating two people who are so pleasing, they give off no sense of wanting to win at all.

When Jane goes to "see a guy about a horse," Charlie slips his hand into his pocket and pulls out a diamond ring in a box for my approval. It is a simple, yet elegant ring with a rather large marquise diamond. She will undoubtedly say yes.

"Is it too soon?" Charlie whispers. "I'm always rushing into things. I can't wait like other people."

"You can ask her next week, next month, next year. The result will be the same."

He is confused.

"She'll say yes, I mean."

"Oh, marvelous. Are you sure?"

"Couldn't be more sure."

Charlie, convinced, taps the box back into his pocket. A huge smile fills his face. "That's all I need to know. I will ask her next week. Or maybe tomorrow."

Jane emerges from the restroom, her makeup refreshed. Charlie leaps to his feet at the sight of her.

The way Charlie is lit up, I decide it is best if I leave.

I offer my thanks for the lovely evening, then say good night to the nearly-engaged and the feline now sleeping on the sofa.

It is a bit beneath me, but I stand outside the closed door until I hear the words, "My dear Jane, I have an important question for you. . ."

I quickly take the steps down to my truck, leaving that special moment between just the two of them.

First Charlotte. Now Jane.

So fast.

As for me, I do not know how to heal. Everything I see around me is another reminder that Darcy is not here. I allow myself to get online once in a while and chat with Georgiana, but school is in full swing now, so I feel as though I am intruding. And, no matter how much I want to, I cannot bring myself to question her about her brother. Not once does she tell me, "Will says hi," or "Will asked about you," or anything else I can hold onto. Only once does she even mention Darcy, saying something off-handedly about her worries over his recent case of writer's block. Then she abruptly changes the subject, as though she had accidentally stepped over a line she had not meant to cross.

It has been a whole month of silence. That silence feels like indifference, or even antipathy. I cannot bear it. Was that "goodbye" Darcy gave me a *forever* goodbye? Oh, what have I done?

I call my father. "How could I ever expect Darcy to feel the same way about me again? I don't deserve him, but I can't just let him go."

My father listens to my dilemma. "Just have patience," he tells me.

That is the last thing I want to hear. I just want to take a Rip Van Winkle nap, then wake up far in the future where everything is different.

Chapter 16

Kate de Bourgh storms into the library.

She points a menacing finger in the air and settles it on me. "You!"

I stand up. "What can I help you with, Mrs. de Bourgh?" I ask, hoping this is going to be a civil conversation, but highly doubting it.

"Come with me!"

Jane looks at me, a question on her face. I shrug my shoulders because I cannot imagine what I might have done to Kate, either. All the librarians are staring at me. A few patrons as well, no doubt, are wondering what I did to set off Kate's wrath.

I reluctantly follow Kate into The Brink Room.

She slams the door closed behind us. Then she starts walking around me in circles, her designer shoes clicking out her irritation.

"What is this I hear about you and William Darcy?!" she spits out.

I am confounded. "Darcy and *me*? I cannot imagine what you may have heard."

"There is a rumor circulating all over Hertford that *you*, a *hick* librarian, are secretly dating Will Darcy."

I take a moment to rewire my brain. "Wait—who is saying this? I haven't heard a word about it."

"Don't pretend to be ignorant of it!"

"I'm telling you honestly, I don't know what you are talking about."

She finally looks at me, her eyes afire with spite. The long wrinkles on her forehead tell me her Botox injection is overdue. "So, it's *not* true?"

"I can't see it would be any of your business if it were or weren't."

Kate's Idaho twang grows more pronounced the more agitated she becomes. "*My business?* You know without a doubt that my daughter Anne is in a relationship with Will Darcy. That makes it *my business.*"

"If that is the truth, there's no reason why he would be seeing me."

"Stubborn girl! Tell me once and for all, are you *dating Darcy?*"

Clearly, she is not going to be rational. I do not think I will leave this room alive without telling her the truth. "*No.* I'm not dating Darcy."

Kate searches my face for signs of deception, then visibly relaxes. "I can firmly contradict the whole of Hertford, then. I have your word?"

"Yes."

"And, can you promise me that you never will?"

I owe no one in the world that much. I step closer. "I will do *no such thing.*"

Her face flushes red with anger. "But. . ."

"*No.* I'm done letting you insult me. I have a job to do. Excuse me."

And, I leave her fuming in The Brink Room.

I am supposed to be leading the discussion for the book club today, but my mind is too full for conversation and I keep staring out the window instead. This is appropriate, since we are discussing *The Secret*

Life of Walter Mitty, a story where the protagonist is a daydreamer. Jane, Charlie, and the rest of the members in the club jabber on about the imaginary lives of this one peculiar character.

I have lived a million lives myself by reading books. I have battled windmills and walked in circles around the smallest planet in the universe. I have fallen in love multiple times with the likes of Gilbert Blythe. I have known the utter loss of a friend who was simply trying to cross into Terabithia. I have fought to hold onto an estate called Pemberley. Stories have been my great comfort through the very real pains of life.

One book I recall reading over and over as a child is *The Practical Princess*. She was the kind of princess that did not wait to be rescued. She did not let timidity get in the way of her goal: she wanted the prince, so she went out and snagged him. I liked her spunk, her initiative. She inspired me to tell Don Samuels that I liked him when I was nine. (It did not go well, but my assertiveness was refreshing.) I learned from *The Practical Princess* that you cannot wait for love to come to you. You must go and you must *get it*. This is a lesson I realize I have forgotten.

I interrupt Jane's spiel about Walter Mitty as a metaphor for. . .whatever. I am hardly paying attention.

"How much would a plane ticket cost to a place like, say, Sacramento?" I ask Charlie. It takes a moment for him to process my non sequitur, but he amiably gives me a sum.

Jane and Charlie share a furtive glance.

"Thank you. Okay. Okay, folks. Just keep talking," I say, then promptly go back to my daydream.

I pull all my dresser drawers out, one by one, looking for loose change or a whole dollar bill. Mrs. Hill makes a point of sitting in each drawer as I go. I empty the cookie jar. My anxious fingers explore all nooks and crannies and coat pockets. I figure if I combine what I find with my meager savings, I can go to Darcy's next book signing, which I learned from an online search is tomorrow in San Francisco. Distance is nothing when one has a motive.

I just need to get my pile of change to the bank, then head to the tiny travel agency for a discounted trip that includes a flight and a Motel 6.

I throw a few clothes in a duffle bag. Then I rethink them, considering the impression I need to make. I cannot afford to dress like the California girls Darcy is used to. A pang of worry overcomes me that Darcy is *right now* falling in love with another woman and they will one day laugh at that Idahoan girl who turned him down in such an abrasive manner.

Darcy's affection for me might still be unshaken, but I cannot allow myself to feel safe. Another fear strangles me for a moment—what if Darcy brushes me off the way he did John Wickham?

My best dress and high heels seem so plain and frumpy, but they are all I have. Makeup. Pajamas. My unsigned copy of *Pemberley*. And I *cannot* do without the toothbrush. Everything goes in the duffle bag.

I fill up Mrs. Hill's food dishes to overflowing. I look at all the drawers on the floor and tell the kitty, "Don't pee in those while I'm gone."

Meow.

Is that yes or no?

Money. Duffle bag. Go.

I put my truck into gear and head out. I turn onto the main road into town and immediately find myself driving in the middle of the traffic heading toward the East Idaho Fair—minivans loaded with kids and trucks full of cowboys. The road is smooth going for about half a mile. Then the long line of traffic slows to 15 miles an hour.

A potato truck the size of a house is bouncing along, taking up two lanes and the farmer driving it could not care less. Is it really time for spud harvest already? Curse these Idaho idiosyncrasies.

What will I say to Darcy? Will my pride even allow me to say "I was wrong"? I am so tired of the stubborn Liz, spiteful Liz, and judgmental Liz. I am tired of getting in my own way. If I had just let myself see him for who he is from the beginning, how different life would be. Can he forgive me?

My heart skips a beat.

There is something wrong with the potato truck ahead. It is wobbling. Did it blow a tire or two? A curve in road ahead causes the truck to swerve dearly, then tip. An ungodly metallic noise shocks my ears as the side of the truck hits the pavement. The mountain of potatoes in the back pours out all over the road and a cloud of dust envelops the scene of the accident. I pull my truck over to the side of the road and run toward the potato truck. My beating heart calms at the sight of the farmer emerging unscathed from the cab.

Potatoes, potatoes everywhere.

Within a minute, distant sirens start wailing. The man in the minivan in front of me attempts to take a detour across the field next to us. The result is one stuck van and five very unhappy kids.

It is *force majeure*, as my father would say: an "act of God." I simply am not meant to get on that airplane today. My urge to do *something* clashes with my inability to act at this moment. My helplessness peaks and leaves me numb.

I pull a blanket out of the cab and tug the rusty tailgate open. I lay the blanket down in the bed of the truck, and climb on top. A breeze, full of the smell of burning weeds and the coming winter, slides across me. My whole body goes limp.

Then I weep. I weep until the sun touches the top of a nearby silo.

I must have fallen asleep.

The first thing I realize is the breeze is now chilly and my face takes the brunt of it. My torso, however, is wonderfully warm. The smell of a splendid, familiar cologne brushes past. I blink a few times and try to make sense of the scene in front of me.

My heart leaps.

Darcy is *here*. He is right in front of me.

In the dimming light, I make out Darcy's handsome, solid profile. The sunset melts behind his sterling form and trails off behind him. He is seated on the edge of the tailgate, his suit pants firmly planted in the dirt. He stares off into the distance.

His black suit jacket is draped across me, explaining the warmth that contains me.

I sit up. My mind swirls with all those words I wanted to say to him, but I cannot say anything.

Darcy turns to look at me. "Liz. You're. . ."

In one swift, decisive move, I slide my arms around him and bury my face in his shoulder.

". . .awake," he finishes. A few excruciating seconds of uncertainty pass, then his arms close around me. I breathe a sigh of relief and pull him in tighter. His touch is secure, dizzying, *perfect*. How I have longed for this closeness.

Several seconds pass as our breathing synchronizes. The chill on my face transforms into a lovely warmth.

I need to say something. I say the first thing my muddled mind can think of. "Will you sign my copy of *Pemberley*?"

His laugh, half surprise and half joy, hums through me. "Sure."

Then his voice is serious. "Is it true, Liz?" he asks.

"Is what true?"

"What Kate de Bourgh told me. She called me to complain about some gossip making its way around Hertford, some rumors concerning a. . .a *relationship* between the two of us. She'd confronted you, and I have *no doubt* made an ugly scene. I suppose she wanted assurance you were telling the truth. Kate was incensed at your defiance, called you some inexcusable names, because you, you. . ."

I sit back and take in the look on his face. His face is a mess of hope, determination, and *fear*.

I brush my pride aside. "I refused *not* to date you? Yes."

His breath quickens. "It gave me hope. More hope than I'd scarcely allowed myself to feel these past couple months. I had to come here; I *had* to see you."

Darcy chokes on his words. His face conveys his struggle, the one I am guilty of causing him. He is putting everything on the line. He says, "My feelings and wishes are unchanged. If you still feel the same way about me, please tell me now. Put me out of my misery."

I have no trouble being honest. The words come from the purest place inside me. "My feelings are so different from what they once were. In fact, they are quite the opposite."

Darcy's demeanor instantly transforms. The fear is gone. In its place is a reassuring warmth that shines out through his eyes.

In this moment, we suddenly appear to be at a loss for words. We sit quietly, simply regarding each other, basking in the freedom of beautiful truths.

A metallic voice on megaphone interrupts. "It's time to move!"

One half the road ahead has been cleared of potatoes and some crewmen are starting to wave my line of cars through.

"You must allow me," I state now my head is clearing, "to thank you for what you did for Lydia." I am anxious to get out the words I have so longed to say. "She does not understand what you did or that anything was really done."

Darcy looks at me, surprise on his face. He did not want me to know about his involvement in Lydia's rescue, but since I do, he cannot deny it.

"I did it for you," he says most pointedly. "I could not bear that you blamed yourself for her predicament."

I manage, slowly, "I suspect, also, that you played a part in Jane's current state of *utter* bliss. How can any of us make amends to you?"

"Lydia and Jane owe me nothing. I confess I only thought of you—your comfort, your happiness."

My eyes flood with tears again. Am I dreaming? Is this *real*?

Megaphone voice says, "Move along!"

The guy in the car behind us honks his horn.

I push the tears back and make a decision. "Come closer so I can tell you something," I say.

Darcy leans in a few inches from my face.

I whisper, "It's time to move."

Then I take Darcy's face in both hands and kiss him. *And* kiss him. And he is *definitely* kissing me back.

Our lips just melt together with an intense energy that slides through every limb. Quick, then slow. Warm, tingly. My hands move through his hair in gentle gestures. Oh, my gosh. There is nothing like kissing the man you want.

Horns start blaring. The line of cars behind us begins to move around my truck. The driver behind me hurls some angry words.

A potato thuds against the side of the truck.

"Wait," I say when we finally come up for air. "How did you find me? Really—why are you here on *this road* right now?"

"After Kate called me, I cancelled my book signings for the coming week. I was heading to Hertford and I saw your truck sitting here."

It is then I notice his red Volvo parked clear down the road, maybe a dozen cars behind mine. What are the chances we are here at the same time, same place?

Fate. Divine intervention. *Force majeure.*

The line of cars disappears, leaving a cloud of potato dust to settle around us.

Darcy puts his head in his hands. He says, "You were so *emphatic* in your refusal to go out with me, I didn't let myself hope you'd change your mind."

"I was unforgivably rude. I can't tell you how much I've regretted it and wanted to tell you."

He lifts his head. His brown eyes sparkle with amusement. "You called me a prick."

I do not remember that one. "If I did, it was under my breath, so it doesn't count."

He laughs. "It *was* under your breath. So, I guess you're forgiven. Can you forgive me?"

"For what?"

He carefully searches for the words. "I *did* treat you like an inferior. My parents, God bless them, raised me with good principles, but also led me to believe I was above others. I've let that pride govern me too much. I'd never really thought about it until you."

I lean in and rest my head on his shoulder. "Oh, why must you smell so good? It isn't fair. Do me a favor and roll in some manure."

He laughs. "*Idahoans.* You're such a peculiar bunch."

"Oh, no. I see I messed up your sideburns when, you know. . ." I go to smooth them down.

"Leave them. You can mess them up as much as you like." He pulls his jacket back up and around my shoulders. "So, I'm here for a week. Our first date—where do you want to go?"

It is funny. Even looking into Darcy's gorgeous eyes, wrapped up in the most perfect moment of my life, with all that relief and joy moving through me, I realize something.

I still want to tease Darcy.

Chapter 17

Square dancing is such a hoot. I wonder why I have not done it in so long. Yet, here we are at Hertford Hall, ready to kick up our heels. I am ready, at least.

Darcy looks suitably uncomfortable at the sight of the "squares" of eight dancers each, moving to twangy music. The "caller," a man in Wranglers and cowboy boots, stands at the front and says "promenade" into the mic. The dancers grab the hands of their partners and start going in a circle to the right.

"Hey," I nudge Darcy. "At least we're not dancing in a barn this time. You won't get too much crap on your shoes here."

Darcy, wearing khakis and a button-down shirt, could almost fit in with the locals, if it were not for the polished shoes. I make a mental note to scuff them up before the night is over.

Our appearance together immediately causes a stir.

"That's William Fitz," someone says in not-so-hushed tones.

"*Told you* those two were dating," another voice says behind us.

Darcy and I look at each other. Our cheeks flush at the same time. It is glorious.

I recognize so many people who frequent the library. That is one of the perks of having a public job. Mr. Lucas says hello and tips his cowboy hat at the two of us.

The floor is a lively swirl of dancers—men in cowboy apparel, women in wide skirts.

"I rarely dance," Darcy explains as he surveys the hall.

"Don't worry about it. Even savages can dance."

"Are you sure about that?" Darcy then points out Collin across the room.

The caller says "do sa do," and Collin tries to go right around his partner instead of left, nearly head-butting her. Charlotte, who is not part of the square itself, steps in and tenderly guides Collin back the correct direction. She looks up, sees me, and waves. Then she goes back to watching her husband obliviously attempting the wrong moves as the others in the square roll their eyes.

"Okay. I might have been wrong," I tell Darcy. "But I have faith in *you*."

I spend a few minutes explaining the basic steps to Darcy. Mr. Lucas comes up and invites us into a new square that is forming.

"Come on, partner," I say and pull Darcy to his spot.

As a group, we clarify which couples are the "heads" and the "sides." I grab the edges of my wide skirt and get ready to dance. As the music starts and the caller begins to give commands, I can tell Darcy is talking himself through the steps as he goes. However, within a few minutes, his stiff under-confidence gives way to elegance.

When the caller says "flutterwheel," the move requires that Darcy and I and the couple opposite meet in the middle, and with a swift twirl find ourselves paired off with the other side's partner. I look at my temporary partner, a cowboy with mud smeared on his pants. He is the kind of boy I grew up with—friendly, humble, hardworking. He gives me a scruffy grin and I respond in kind, just without the scruff.

The dark-haired girl now paired with Darcy is a good foot shorter than he. A glance at her face tells me she finds the height difference entertaining. I breathe a sigh of relief when a move means we return to our original partners.

The dance is series of pairing and separating, touching and releasing. I ache during each separation for that brief touching of hands. The eye contact between Darcy and me is our constant connection. His amusement is my amusement. His touch is mine too.

It is five minutes of twangy sexiness.

Once the dance ends, everyone in the square shakes hands.

Darcy and I pause to check out the refreshment table. Charlotte is there, busily filling up plastic cups with punch.

"Mr. Darcy," says Collin, running over to greet him. "You're welcome to our little shindig."

"Thank you, sir," Darcy says. He shakes Collin's hand, then reaches over to take mine.

When Collin sees Darcy's hand wrap around mine, he takes a step back. He processes the action for a few moments. He surmises, "Ah, I see this is something of a date for the two of you."

"It is," I say.

Darcy and I look at each other, tacitly agreeing this could be an uncomfortable situation, considering Collin's employer. Our hands clasp more tightly.

Luckily, Collin aims for diplomatic. "May the night be pleasant. . ."

His phone rings. He whips it out and says, "Five minutes, ma'am."

Charlotte looks up from the punch, "You must be off, dear. Don't forget to come back and get me this time."

"Excuse me," says Collin, then takes off with alarming speed, almost knocking a woman over on the way out the door.

"Punch? Cookies?" Charlotte asks.

A chocolate chip cookie beckons. And so does its friend.

Darcy is a step ahead of me. He stacks two cookies on a napkin and presents them to me.

"A man after my own heart," I say. I bite into a cookie and it is insanely delicious. Charlotte has outdone herself again.

Darcy pauses over the refreshments, trying to decide. A woman sways her way up to Darcy and taps him on the shoulder. Her big hair and short skirt tell me she is on the prowl.

"Excuse me, sir," she says in a startling, high-pitched voice. "We have a shortage of men here tonight. I don't suppose you'd be willing to be my partner for the next dance?" She looks Darcy up and down, pleased with what she sees.

I want to give her my best "hands off" look, but my mouth is full of cookie and I am sure all she sees is "chipmunk face."

The next song begins. The woman grabs Darcy by the arm and pulls him toward the nearest square. Darcy looks at me desperately. I know how these Idahoan women can be. They are good at hunting animals and men equally.

"That's what happens when you've been dancing with the only handsome man in the room," Charlotte tells me. Then she goes back to arranging treats on the table.

Darcy walks uncomfortably through the motions of the dance and ignores the flirty glances and touches the woman throws at him. She very brazenly moves in close even when the dance move does not call for it. In obvious "accidental" moves, she puts her hands on his chest or rubs his arm. I start to wonder if she is related to Lydia.

To give Darcy some credit, he stays one step ahead of her and makes no show of accepting her flirtations.

Darcy just sees me.

Even from across the room, our eyes are still connected, our souls perfected in the invisible transference between us. How my feelings for him have changed. My hope is tentative, the flame of love delicate.

My mind sweeps away every other person in the room. There are only two of us here, suspended in the artful web dreams create.

I can sense one fact flowing into me: Darcy is *all mine*.

The song seems to go on *way too long*. I eat four cookies while I wait impatiently. When I can tell the song is nearly over, I gulp down some punch and head over to reclaim my man.

Darcy exits the square a few beats before the end of the song, leaving the woman stunned. She tries to go after him, but it is too late.

In a few strides, he moves in front of me. Darcy's height awes me as he draws close. He motions toward me, and for a moment I think he is going to whisper something in my ear, but at the last second his lean-in changes course. His soft lips find mine. He kisses me with an intensity that leaves my legs shaky. Instinctively, my arms wrap around him, pulling us closer. And the kissing just keeps going.

Wow. That's all I can think: *wow*.

The surprise of the impromptu make-out session makes me forget Darcy and I are kissing in front of a room *full of people*.

I open my eyes a smidgen and spot Darcy's former dance partner glaring at me over his shoulder. She should no longer have a doubt who Darcy is with tonight.

Whispers start, then grow louder around us. Soon clapping and little whoops ignite in every corner of the room. Ah, the gossip that will follow us around Hertford from this night on. Who cares? Just kiss me again, Darcy.

"That's eight seconds!" Mr. Lucas says, and everyone laughs.

So do we. Darcy and I finally step apart as the next song begins.

Charlotte raises an eyebrow at me as I wipe off my mouth. I should be embarrassed, but I do not feel it. I might need another glass of punch to cool myself down, however.

"Dance with me?" Darcy asks.

I wipe the bit of lipstick off his face and smooth down a sideburn before we join another square far from the big-haired woman who now is making her moves on the second handsomest man in the room. I can still feel her sharp and vengeful glare.

After Darcy and I exhaust ourselves with a few more dances, we say good night to Charlotte, and step outside the hall.

The cool September air hits, stinging my face. It seems a bit early for a scarf, but I came prepared. I stop to wrap it around my neck.

As we are standing there, Darcy notices a piece of paper tucked into his jacket pocket. He unfolds the curious object.

"Huh. Caroline wants me to call her," Darcy says. He shows me the paper with her name and number and a little heart.

That sneaky, big-haired witch. I wondered why she was standing so close to Darcy on his way out.

I snatch the paper from Darcy's fingers. "Caroline can jump off a cliff."

I see a man standing alone in the smoking area. I march over and hand him the paper. "Have fun."

He takes the paper, glances over it, and gives me a thumbs up.

Darcy opens the passenger side door of his car for me. (*Sigh.*) What a gentleman. Chivalry is not dead; it has been in another state this whole time.

I scoot inside.

Just as Darcy gets in and puts on his seatbelt, his phone rings.

"Don't tell me 'Caroline' somehow got your number?" I say, possibly with a hint of jealousy.

"That's a negative." He rejects the call. "It's Kate de Bourgh. No doubt *someone* told her he saw us together tonight."

"I don't care what she or anyone else thinks."

Darcy smiles. "Neither do I," he says as he starts the car.

With the music from the dance hall still pounding in my head, my need to talk diminishes. Instead I look out the window as I snatch at random thoughts floating around in my mind.

I consider the fact that Darcy and I just had our first date. There were a few awkward moments and a certain pesky temptress to deal with, but overall I would say it was success. Compared to tonight, my whole dating life feels like a string of first dates ranging from mediocre to Collin-awful.

I wonder how Darcy is feeling about the matter, but he is as quiet as I am. It is not that awkward, sometimes rude silence that means two people are avoiding a confrontation. It seems to me we are both just analyzing the moment, the potential steps we can take from here.

As we exit the town, we pass the Supreme Spuds factory with its foggy output billowing from the stacks. We wave at Mr. Lucas as he rides Goober back to his farm. A sign reminds us to turn around and get our free tater at the Potato Museum. We travel past fields, tractors, a group of trucks involved in a tailgate party complete with bonfire.

Then suddenly a nauseating stench fills the car.

Oh, no, Idaho. *Not now.*

My gag reflex triggers, but I fight it back.

I am used to these "surprises." All Idahoans are. One whiff and we can say "potato farm," "dairy farm," "backed-up sewage tank," "Uncle Joe." This stink is definitely cow in origin.

The horrid smell permeates the interior of Darcy's cherry Volvo. What *did* those cows eat? Should I roll down the window?

Oh, gosh. My eyes are watering. I glance at Darcy who is now blinking and trying to hold a straight face.

And now the quiet seems suspicious. Does Darcy think I am responsible for this smell? Does he not yet understand about cows? Maybe he thinks that *I* think he is to blame, but that is impossible. I am sure Darcy never farts.

"Windows," I say, finally breaking the silence. We each hit the buttons and a swoosh of outside air comes in, but it is just as bad as the air inside.

We start coughing and laughing at the same time.

"It was a great night," Darcy says, coughing between words.

"Despite the dancing?"

"Yes."

"And the crazy chick?"

"Yes."

"And the malodorous reminder of where we are?"

"Actually, I think this is a nice touch," Darcy says, and tries to wave the smell away. "If I ever need to write a scene on a dairy farm, I have no illusions."

Dairy farm? I weirdly love that he got it right.

We pull into my driveway. The air is starting to clear, but it is not there yet. Darcy puts the car into park.

He turns to me, takes my hand.

"Would you have dinner with me tomorrow night, Ms. Liz?" Darcy asks. I adore the gentle yearning in his face.

No need to think about it. "Yes."

"Good. I will pick you up at 6. We have a bit of a drive."

Huh? Oh, well. I am curious, but not alarmed.

Darcy gets out.

The idling of the car hums as I wait. I sit, content to keep letting Darcy open doors for me.

Georgiana sends me a message while I am out with her brother.

Georgiana: *It's about time!! I've been telling him to try again for weeks. Amazing what a little hope can do.*

P.S. I've always wanted a sister. (hint, hint)

"When is it going to be *my* turn?" Kitty grumbles upon hearing about my date with Darcy.

Mary pulls out one of her antique etiquette books and locates a list of courting rules that probably make sense only to her and everyone's great-great grandmother. I let her explain to me how there should be no touching until after ten times of "walking out" together and only when my father is present to make sure it does not go too far. I listen carefully, then promptly call Darcy so I can "mess up his sideburns" during my lunch break.

Jane is delighted by the news, of course. For once I find myself sharing her romantic glow rather than feeling keenly the contrast between her happiness and my own despair. It is an added joy to share with my good friend.

Mrs. Bennet does not speak to me for nearly a full work day once the news breaks about my date with Darcy. She walks smugly around the library for a while, taking great pains not to glance in my direction. She sits next to her husband, complains about her nerves, and when he shows no sympathy, she moves on. By lunchtime, she starts to open up to the other patrons and, finally, the librarians. When we are preparing to close up for the day, she congratulates me and assures me that she knew Darcy was the man for me the first time she saw him.

Even when Mrs. Young pulls me aside to explain that Kate de Bourgh has called multiple times in a desperate attempt to get me fired, my spirits remain calm and sure. I cannot bear to be frightened at the will of others. My courage rises at this attempt to intimidate me. Now, with Darcy at my side, I have no doubt I will get through the storm.

"What do you call four tractors surrounding a McDonald's?" a man in a suit asks during a business dinner. He pauses for effect, then answers his own question: "Prom night in Idaho."

The group of formally dressed men and women around him laugh, then tuck into their gourmet desserts.

Darcy struggles not to laugh. That is the third Idaho joke I have had to listen to as Darcy and I wait for our meal. We are at Chez Guillaume, a reservations-only upscale restaurant in Salt Lake City.

I look around the restaurant, its velvet curtains and crystal chandelier. A bizarre arrangement of silverware with three forks and three spoons hypnotizes me. I am wearing a denim skirt and Goodwill sweater. I feel as out-of-place as Darcy felt on square-dancing night.

Touché, Darcy.

I try the lobster Darcy forced me to order despite my objections over the price. The lobster basically melts in my mouth. The live classical violin music reaches through me and my soul begins to sway to its beauty. In the candlelight, Darcy's eyes flicker between soft and intense.

Our conversation tonight is predictably more subdued than it was during square dancing. Once Darcy lets down his guard, there is a whole inner world to explore. He suffered through bouts of pain and intense doubt as he struggled to become a published author. The memories of his parents and their desire to see him succeed pushed him to keep trying until *Pemberley* found a publisher. At the same time, he does not seem to believe he deserves any of his own triumphs, as though anything he accomplishes is simply an extension of his parents' achievements and not his own.

Like a true gentleman, he wants to learn about me, as well. He lets me talk. He listens without judgment as I describe the life of a lonely girl who found books to be better friends than people. We discuss my quirky father, an injured soul who never failed to tell his daughter he was proud of her.

Darcy's phone buzzes, but he ignores it. He says, "I blocked Kate on my phone, but it hasn't stopped her from calling from other lines. She came pounding on my door late last night too."

"You mean to tell me her obsessive, crazy behavior doesn't make you want to marry her daughter?"

"Not at all."

"But Kate would be the *ideal* mother-in-law. You should take a few minutes, reconsider. . ."

He smiles. "All right, I will. *Hmm.* The answer is still a firm *no.*"

"Now tell me about the book you're writing," I say, hoping for a tidbit. I give him my innocent look, but he is not swayed.

He laughs. "I'm afraid you will have to read it along with everyone else."

"I don't want to know *everything.* I just want to know who is in it, what they say and do, how it all ends, and every detail in between."

"Nice try." He shakes his head.

"But Thomas. . ."

"I'm Darcy."

"Of course, I know that. It's just. . . How's Thomas? Is he okay? I worry about him all the time."

He pauses and blinks twice. "You know he is not real, right?"

Neither is Santa Claus, I tell myself, but my heart does not understand it. I feel like a lunatic, but still say, "I *want* to believe that. I do. Tom just *feels* so real."

"Tom?"

"I gave him a nickname. We're that close." Oh, gosh. I *am* a lunatic. I cannot distinguish between fiction and reality at all. "He's just so well-written. You could say I found a friend in your book."

Darcy gives me an embarrassed smile, then says, "Thank you for that. What do you think of the lobster? Would you like some dessert?"

"*Okay.* I see you're trying to change the subject. At least tell me the title. Then I'll leave you alone."

"No," he says, but the look in his eyes is playful.

"Okay. I will guess. Is it *Pemberley, the Sequel?*"

"What a prosaic, unappealing title."

"So, *that's* not it. *Crime and Pemberley?*"

"Dostoevsky already used that."

"*Pemberley and Zombies?*"

He crinkles his nose. "Heavens, *no*."

"Wait. I know. It's *Fifty Shades of Pemberley*."

Darcy's eyes narrow as he considers that one. "That might be it. Explain to me what happens in that novel."

"The owner of Pemberley finds a mysterious key. He discovers it fits in an attic door he has never entered. Inside the attic, he encounters a crazy lady whose husband locked her up years before. After living in the dark for so long, she insists on leaving on every lamp in the manor."

"Let me guess. There are fifty lamps with fifty shades."

"I haven't quite worked out the details, but that sounds about right."

"*Not* what I was expecting." He chuckles for a moment, then dabs at his mouth with his napkin.

I offer, "I can add some knickers to make it a better story."

"Why don't *you* write the story and I'll read it."

"Deal." And, I continue yakking, mentioning Camus—my ultimate test of a man's intelligence—and Darcy does not miss a beat. We discuss *The Stranger* all through our chocolate soufflé.

Nothing sexier than a man who knows his books.

Why, kitty? *Why?* Must you sit on *every blasted book* I want to read?

I move Mrs. Hill and snatch *Bridget Jones's Diary* back.

She hisses.

Enough. I pick her up, toss her out of the bedroom, and shut the door.

A period of quiet, Mrs. Hill's version of "the silent treatment," lasts less than a minute. This is followed by ten minutes of her impatient meow—a squeaky, angry sound. I am used to ignoring this sound. I can read, undeterred, the story of Bridget and *her* Mr. Darcy, awestruck at the similarities between her story and my own.

However, it is the next kind of meow—the kittenish, "repentant" meow—that interferes with my thoughts.

Meow. It is soft, pure-hearted. *Meow.*

The delicate mewing evokes memories of how I came to adopt Mrs. Hill. It was I who found her in the book drop box after some prankster slipped her through the slot at Longbourn Library. She was so tiny then, her big brown eyes seemingly too large for her head. I placed her on a shelf under the checkout desk. All day she purred at me with appreciation mixed with admiration.

Her little meows let me know she wanted another scratch on the back and soon she was sleeping on my shoulder, a picture of all that is innocent and cozy.

At the end of the day I volunteered to adopt her. Of course I did.

I brought her home and named her Mrs. Hill because I was reading a Grace Livingston Hill novel at the time. My cat was cute *then*.

Meow. It pulls at my heartstrings.

Meow. A pause follows that seems *so* sad, as though she is close to giving up her one heart's desire: having an open door.

I feel guilty. *Meow.*

I cave. I open the door to a little cat face, now with an angelic halo hanging over it. She eyes the bed.

Instantly, her whole demeanor changes back to "demon Mrs. Hill." She races to the bed and leaps onto my book, covering it with her whole body. She *owns* it. Her eyes dare me to tell her otherwise.

"I am going to cuddle with someone else from now on," I inform her in all honesty.

Hiss.

"Tell me again." The words are muffled because my face is buried in Darcy's shoulder.

"I'm coming back in two weeks."

"You can't make it sooner?"

"I would if I could."

The slam of books on a nearby desk makes me jump. "No kissing in the library," Mary sternly reminds us.

I say into Darcy's shoulder, "I know, Mary. I wasn't planning to."

Darcy whispers, "I was."

"We all know you were," comes a loud whisper from the other side of the shelf. It is Mrs. Bennet, once again pretending to need a book right next to us.

Sheesh. No privacy at all.

The week has gone by far too quickly for Darcy and me. We danced, we dined, we stayed in for a movie. Yesterday Jane and Charlie joined us for a double date to Craters of the Moon park. With every moment I spent with Darcy, my fondness and surety grew. We forgave each other the stubbornness that kept us apart.

With a final hug and a sneaky kiss on the forehead, Darcy says, "I will be here in two weeks' time, Liz. Nothing could keep me from it."

Parting is such sweet sorrow. That is the Shakespeare line that hits me as Darcy makes a final wave goodbye and exits Longbourn

Library. First, I feel the sweet assurance that he will return, then the dreadful pang of sorrow that he is gone.

This time Darcy's absence is different. There is no gigantic question mark hanging in the air, making me doubt if we have a chance. I wander through my day at Longbourn Library, seeing the books inside in a new light. All those shelves of romance novels are no longer just reflections of my inner hopes, but representations of my own story.

I am the heroine for once. And Will Darcy is my hero.

Chapter 18

I cannot go a whole day without seeing Darcy's face. As soon as he finishes his latest reading in Denver, we set up a video chat.

Mrs. Hill hisses at Darcy's face the first time she sees him on screen.

"Don't rely on your first impressions of the man," I tell my cat as she growls.

Darcy laughs. "I hope *she* improves on better acquaintance as well."

I scratch Mrs. Hill on the top of the head until she starts to relax. "She is fiercely loyal once she makes up her mind that she trusts you."

"Something to aim for."

Confession time. "Every librarian in the world has a cat. Sometimes two, three. Just FYI."

"So, you two are a package deal?"

Meow.

I interpret. "That means yes."

"Duly noted."

We discuss his on-going book tour, the latest Tuesday Tea catastrophe (Mary *tried* to sing, *again*), and, the most recent development in the Kate de Bourgh war.

"She resigned," I tell Darcy. "And not quietly."

Kate hoped the town would rally around her when she threatened to quit her job. Only her faithful servant Collin made any kind of fuss

166

about the matter, and in the end it was not enough. When it became clear no one was going to picket the library in her honor, Kate resigned by telling everyone off who had ever looked at her the wrong way. The library staff simply breathed a sigh of relief after years of dealing with such a diva.

I took down the colored blob painting in celebration.

Despite the joy of being relieved of Kate, I worry what Collin's job loss will mean for Charlotte. I feel responsible.

"It's not your fault, Liz. You didn't do anything wrong," Darcy assures me. It is as though he can read my deepest feelings and fears.

I take his words to heart. Kate's choices are hers alone.

"I refuse to regret you, Darcy. I *never* will, no matter what happens or who disapproves." I am pushing myself to be more honest, more forthcoming about my feelings. It is not easy.

He sits back in his chair, regarding me with keen consideration. "I realize this is sudden," he says, "perhaps too soon, but you must allow me to tell you how much I admire and love you."

My heart thumps. Tears form. I reach up and touch the screen, wishing it were his princely face.

"I love you too."

Lady Ambrosia and Prince Porkchop, now a married team, discover a treasure map promising the treasure of Sultan Scorpion. They travel to a bridge, but a magic camel tells them they must answer a question about *The Arabian Nights* to cross.

"Have you read *The Arabian Nights*?" Lady Ambrosia asks her audience. A few kids nod their heads. "It is a wonderful book, full of magical stories. Luckily, Prince Porkchop and I have read *every book* in

Kitty's Korner."

The lady turns to the camel. "Ask us the question," she tells him with courage.

Denny's low camel voice says, "What did Ali Baba say to open the cave?"

"He said, 'Open Sesame!'" replies Lady Ambrosia.

"That is correct. You may pass." The camel puppet trots off the stage.

The prince and the lady follow the treasure map to a gate guarded by a snake puppet. This time it is Kitty's slithery voice: "Ansssswer thisss quessstion to open the gate: What isss inssside Aladdin'sss lamp?"

Prince Porkchop asks the audience for help. One little boy shouts, "A genie!"

"Oh, I think that is it. Miss Snake, is it *a genie*?"

"That isss correct." And, so the journey continues.

They make a great team, Kitty and Denny. Their on-stage banter seems less forced, less of a "job" these days. Their silly voices crack everyone up.

Lady Ambrosia and Prince Porkchop, with audience help, answer each question, dealing with each obstacle until at last they open the sultan's treasure box.

And, the treasure? A library card: key to all the doors in the story world.

Darcy is tense and inarticulate on the way to Boise. He has been more like his old self all day. I assure Darcy my father is a good soul, but he still clams up.

I tell him, "Ask my father about his leg; he'll tell you a bloody war story and soon you'll feel right at home. You can call him Stumpy."

Darcy looks more terrified than ever.

Finally, we arrive at the care facility in Boise. I pull Darcy into my father's room. "Stumpy" greets us with his gap-toothed smile. I notice he is wearing his best overalls.

"Will you do me the honor of introducing me to your father?" Darcy asks me.

"Dad, this is Mr. William Darcy."

"A pleasure to meet you, young man." Darcy steps forward and they shake hands. My father looks Darcy up and down. I know from the twinkle in my father's eyes that Darcy's tailored suit is as funny to him as it once was to me.

My father tells me, "Leave me alone with this young man, Lizzie. Don't worry, the shotgun is loaded."

"Sure enough. Make sure he's still got a couple limbs left, will you, Daddy?"

Darcy gives me half a grimace that I think was meant to be a smile.

I pace the halls of the facility for over an hour. I am struck by how correct Charlotte was when she told me "things change so quickly." I would not have thought a few months ago that I would be completely in love with the man I despised so much back then: arrogant, stiff, implacable, preening, prick-ish Darcy—that perfectly amazing man. He is what I need in both temper and intelligence. He answers all the wishes I have in my heart.

What could Darcy and my father be talking about? Finally, curiosity gets to me and I crack open the door to the room.

My father is holding his fake leg above his head, twirling it around.

"Dad!" I yell. He always plays with his fake leg as though it is a toy he just got for Christmas. Heaven forbid he ends up with two.

"Hi, sweetie. Darcy and I are just having a laugh." My father's grin takes up half his face.

"It's true," Darcy tells me. He seems at ease and genuinely amused by my father's shenanigans.

Then my father's smile suddenly disappears. The instant seriousness on his face is unnerving.

He turns to Darcy. "Now that Lizzie is here, it is time to have an important discussion, Mr. Darcy."

Darcy's eyes widen and he sits up straighter.

"Sir?" asks Darcy, immediately very formal and nervous.

My father has never let any of my dates get out the door without a substantial ribbing, so I can guess the nature of what is coming, but Darcy cannot.

"William Darcy," my father says slowly, looking him up and down. "It has come to my attention that you enjoy my daughter's company."

"That is true, sir."

"Could one say you like her very much?"

Darcy looks at me tenderly. "Very, very much. I love her, most ardently." He holds out his hand toward me, and I take it without thinking. We are a couple.

"Ah." My father scratches his chin like a scientist making an astute assessment. "Then it seems we need to come to an arrangement."

Darcy gives me a "What's going on?" look. I keep my face

serious, playing along with whatever the joke may be this time.

My father continues, "In light of your admission, Mr. Darcy, I must make a request."

"What is it, sir?" Darcy asks, bewildered.

The fake leg goes back on. The overalls get straightened. My father's face remains severe and icy. I can feel Darcy's palm getting sweaty.

With eyes directed straight into Darcy's, my father finally speaks. "I need a grandchild."

Darcy's jaw drops.

"*Dad!!*" I scream.

My father's huge smile comes back. "Actually, I'm thinking grand*children*—two, three. . ."

"What the. . .? *Dad!*"

"Why not get them all out at once? *Twins?*"

He is supposed to be teasing *Darcy*, not *me*. A fresh surge of anger rises. I have had enough.

"For crying out loud, Stumpy, grow your own grandchildren!"

Darcy's façade of formality breaks. He starts to chuckle along with my father.

They are laughing and I am pissed off. The redder I get, the harder my father laughs. I hit him on the shoulder repeatedly.

My father says, "Okay, okay. *Triplets.* They'll all be named Darcy. Will that do?"

"*Unbelievable!!!*" I cross my arms like a petulant child. My father rubs his shoulder, but I know he cannot be hurting too much.

Darcy hugs me and kisses my forehead as I boil. "Liz wants us to change the subject," he says.

My father winks at me.

And the two of them go back to talking like old friends.

I remember now why Darcy's mother seemed familiar to me. The reason came to me in the middle of the night, a sudden ghostly wisp floating in through my window. The recall came on words both haunting and lovely stirring in the recesses of my memory.

I was a young girl, sullen and lonely, when I opened a random book from the shelves of Barnes and Noble. The elaborate, floral cover and the thinness of the book seemed less intimidating to me than so many in the "grown-up" section. So, I cracked open the book and immediately found myself carried away by the poetry within.

The poems wove stories from another world, opened my mind to the music of alliteration a step beyond the usual Dr. Seuss. The strange, abstract images of silver butterflies and tender breezes thrilled me. I found myself reading the words aloud—an act which caused both staff and patrons to stare. It was the first time poetry had really reached into my soul.

I read all afternoon, so immersed in the poetry that coming to the end of the book was unexpected and almost traumatizing. With the words scintillating my thoughts, I turned to the final page and confronted the picture of the poet: a stunning dark-eyed beauty named Regina Darcy.

Charles Dickens said, "You are part of my existence, part of myself. You have been in every line I have ever read."

I feel this way about Darcy. He has been in my blood longer than I could have imagined. Long ago he sneaked in through citrus fruit, poetry, and *Pemberley*.

Chapter 19

"Now, where is Darcy's girlfriend from? Ohio? *Iowa?*" The Californian woman's voice carries into my bathroom stall a little too well.

She rummages through her purse. "Where. . .is. . .my. . .lipstick?"

Another woman speaks up. "No, I think it's Idaho. I think of potatoes whenever I look at her face."

The first woman cackles and responds, "That's not very flattering, dear. Anyway, I knew she was from *somewhere* in the Midwest. She has 'Podunk' written all over her."

Sheesh. Saying Idaho is in the Midwest is like saying California is on the East Coast.

"You know, I watched her eat a huge slice of pumpkin pie like it doesn't have any calories."

What am I supposed to eat—*salad?* It's *Thanksgiving.* I peek through the door gap. Both women at the mirror look as though they have not eaten anything today, or in the past decade.

"Let's just hope there aren't too many of these Idaho women trying to snatch up our men."

"These outsiders are already taking over the state, from what I hear."

At long last, the women finish spackling on their makeup and exit the restroom.

I step out of the stall and startle at my own reflection in the mirror. It is as though I finally got to attend prom. Red velvet dress—*not* from Goodwill. High heels made for dancing. Hair twisted into a masterpiece by a hairdresser named Pei-Hsuen. My heart-shaped diamond necklace—a birthday gift from Darcy—lights up under my touch. Perhaps my face somehow says "tuber dug up from the dirt," but everything else says "*sha-zaam.*"

I admit I hesitated to join Darcy and Georgiana for Thanksgiving here in Sacramento. I said no initially, not wanting to abandon my father for the first time in my whole life. But then my father insisted I go. *Really* insisted.

And then Darcy said the magic words, "Don't worry, we'll stay in Idaho with your father next year."

I was hooked.

Next year.

All this time, I have been taking this relationship one day at a time, worried I would mess up and get the boot, and Darcy has been thinking *next year*, as though we would naturally still be together. How could I not agree to come after that?

So I flew out of my snowy Idaho comfort zone into a California wrapped in warm breezes and punctuated with palm trees.

It turns out California really is an easy distance away.

One more glance in the mirror. Suck in the tummy. On goes an extra layer of some imitation scent I got at Walgreen's because, you know, I cannot get it *all* right.

This "Thanksgiving Gala" in Sacramento includes Darcy, Georgiana, the mayor of Sacramento, and a whole ballroom of allegedly important people. This type of formal gathering is an uncomfortable reminder of my own "humble" roots. I walked into the building and immediately wanted to leave. However, if there is one thing Darcy has taught me, it is we belong wherever our heart is. I belong here, just as much as he belongs in Hertford. I remind myself of that every time another person's judgment, including my own, creeps in.

I put my sexy walk on and head toward Darcy at our table. The ballroom stretches out before me like a movie scene. An orchestra scores my entrance with something up-tempo, almost jazzy. As far as everyone knows, I am a movie star. Better yet, I just stepped out of an Ian Fleming novel, ready to join my James Bond at the table.

Does Darcy *ever* slouch? I can pick him out of a room on his straight back alone. With his back to me, the cut of his tuxedo, the turn of his head and, of course, the sideburns, he reminds me of Laurence Olivier once again. Georgiana, sitting next to him, looks darling in a pale green beaded gown.

I have a speech prepared, a bunch of sweet nothings I plan to whisper into Darcy's ear as soon as I sit down.

With a few more clacks of my high heels, I slide in next to him, lean in toward him, and. . .

"Oooh, chocolate." I grab the nearest fork and dig into the pie in front of me. I shove in a mouthful before I remember myself.

Amusement flashes across Darcy's face. "That is my pie, Liz. Well, *was* my pie."

Georgiana bursts into laughter.

I finish chewing and poke at my mouth with a linen napkin. "I was just testing it for you. It might be poisoned."

"And what's the verdict?"

"Am I dead?"

"No, thank heavens."

"Then it must be okay. Really, I was doing you a favor."

Georgiana chimes in, "Who'd want to poison Will, anyway?"

The corner of Darcy's mouth turns up. He gives me a sweeping glance from head to toe. "I suspect every man in this room would like to kill off the competition."

Blood rushes to my face. I have always had a hard time with compliments as well as confrontation.

Georgiana laughs and hands me her glass of water. "Cool down, Liz. Your face is as red as your dress."

I gulp down the water. The entire glass.

The orchestra starts up a new melody, a waltz.

A young man, tan and dressed to the nines, appears at Georgiana's side. "Care to dance, Miss Darcy?"

Georgiana hesitates a bit and looks to me as though asking "Should I?" She is surprisingly shy at times.

I give her an encouraging nod.

"Thank you, yes," she agrees, then moves onto the dance floor with the man. They join hands and make an elegant circle. They step fluidly in time with the music. Wow. Someone's had dance lessons.

The dance redefines graceful for me. I love the way Georgiana tilts her head back, holds her arms up, back straight, perfectly balanced as her steps glide through the rises and falls. The guy she is dancing with matches her stride with uncanny perfection.

As I watch Georgiana, I ache for her, how John deceived and manipulated her in her moment of most intense grief. However, I see her now stepping up and reclaiming her life. She will be a force for good her whole life, her empathy for others' misfortunes very real.

Georgiana breaks the dance frame as she laughs at something the guy says. She hits him on the arm. He grins. And somehow they manage between giggles to get back into their stance and start again.

I note, "They say that being fond of dancing is the first step toward falling in love."

"I thought it was being fond of reading." Darcy kisses me on the neck and I instantly melt into a red velvet puddle.

"Being fond of reading?" I say as I shake off the tingle of that kiss. "That helps, too, especially in my case. I certainly didn't fall for you based on your square dancing prowess. And you. . ." I search Darcy's face. "You admired my incivility? My impertinence?"

"I prefer to call it liveliness of mind." He moves his glass in front of me. "Here's some more water. Prepare yourself for another compliment."

I swig some down.

Darcy says, "Since my parents forced me to attend this Thanksgiving Gala event every year, I know most of the women here. See the stick insect in black over there? I once asked her if she likes Kazuo Ishiguro, and she replied that she simply adores that *designer.*"

"No!"

Darcy points to another woman, one with oversized, uh, *assets.* "She only reads beauty magazines."

He points to another in impossibly high heels. "She just doesn't like to read because it's 'boring.'"

"*Utter sacrilege.*"

"I recognized long ago I was disgusted with the women who were always speaking and acting for my approval alone. You could say I became interested in you because you were so unlike *them.*" He gestures to the room at large, then continues. "While I was writing *Pemberley,* I realized I needed a different kind of 'sophisticated' than I was used to. I needed intelligence, passion, humor, depth. Granted, the last place I expected to find it was in *Idaho*. But, not long after I met you, Liz, I just *knew*." He pauses, gathering his thoughts. "I *knew* that if I could win your heart, I would never wish to be parted from you from that day on."

The writer in Darcy just knows what to say sometimes.

I slide in closer and put my arms around him, enveloping his suave tuxedo. I never tire of having him close. "You have my heart."

Darcy sits at a writing desk concerning himself with a stack of mail that has been gathering at his Sacramento home. Across the expanse of the lofty, handsome room, Georgiana delicately plays some Chopin on the ornate grand piano.

From the large window, I observe the beauties of the surrounding area: a hill crowned with trees, a small lake positioned down the hill from the house. I spy a Queen Anne gazebo near the lake and I trace a pathway from the house I imagine connects to the gazebo, but the path gets lost in the wooded area, so I cannot be sure.

Mrs. Reynolds, a cheery gray-haired lady fulfilling a lifetime of housekeeping, enters and hands Darcy another document to peruse. He accepts it with a sense of interest and responsibility.

With everyone occupied, I am at leisure to feel a great deal of curiosity, so I decide to take a few minutes to explore. I walked through the house a little as Darcy showed me to my room and so forth, but I have not seen the place in its entirety. To be honest, I am tired of seeing big houses. I find little pleasure in fine carpets or satin curtains. I am far more interested in the promise of a library and that elusive secret passageway I have longed to locate my entire life. And, if I do not find the passageway today, I will check out the wardrobes. I have read great things about the backs of wardrobes.

I tip-toe out of the room and turn down a hallway, which leads to another hallway. Antique French furniture, preserved in near-perfect form, lines the halls. In the second hall, there seems to be a gallery of sorts above the wainscoting. Antique paintings of family peer at me while holding regal poses in decidedly old-fashioned clothing. I skip most of them and walk swiftly in quest of the only faces whose features are known to me. At last they arrest me: James Darcy, with such a smile as Darcy sometimes has when he looks at me, and Regina "Gina" Darcy, the dark-eyed poet with 1980's feathered hair. I step down to Georgiana's portrait, a sweet recent rendition of her in pink lace. Then I stare in earnest contemplation at Darcy wearing the same suit, I swear, straight-backed and serious. He appears to be around 22. I long to tell him to smile.

I continue past room after room—certainly more bathrooms than is humanly needed—to the *library*.

At the sight and smell of all those glorious books, my body instantly starts to bust a move in my "got-a-book dance." I normally reserve this special way of shaking my butt for times when the next book in a series arrives in bookstores. I do a bunch of random cheerleader moves combined with hip-hop twists and turns. I bend down to try something I saw on TV called "twerking."

And. . .I have an audience.

Mrs. Reynolds patters down the hallway past me, pretending to be engrossed in a document at hand. I pause the twerk mid-shake until she passes.

Then I stand and wiggle my way through the doorway into the

library.

The Darcy library is not the marvelous stunner that Belle found in the Beast's castle, but it is nearly half the size of Longbourn Library. I would not complain about anything these bookshelves have to offer. I spy books by Haruki Murakami, Richard Wright, Katherine Ann Porter, Khalil Gibran—further signs of fine taste. A corner filled with children's books such as *The Phantom Tollbooth, How Fletcher was Hatched*, and *The Hardy Boys* collection gives me a peek into the literary influences of Darcy's childhood.

The delightful scents of old books and sturdy oak glide around me as I tiptoe from shelf to shelf. Like Darcy's bookshelves in Hertford, these too are properly organized and filled to perfection.

Several comfy chairs beg me to sit in them for hours with a book propped against an armrest.

I discover far more than a dream collection of books in this tucked-away room. On the wall is a portrait of an ancestor, the clear inspiration for one of my favorite literary characters. The distinguished gentleman, straight-backed in a cutaway coat, practically strides off the canvas. His mouth is firm; an unyielding look in his eyes digs into my soul. His hand grasps a sword at his hip as though he is ready to fight the world. The nameplate on the frame states this is *Thomas Wiley D'arcy*.

"D'arcy"? Simplified to "Darcy" at one point, I decide.

I compare Thomas's portrait to my sole picture of my paternal grandmother, one I keep in my purse at all times—a Polaroid of her holding a huge bass she caught in the Snake River. Her jeans are rolled up to her knees, her gingham shirt tied in a knot at her stomach. She kneels in the mud on the river bank and holds out the silvery, heavy fish. The sassy triumph in her face always said to me "Have fun; enjoy life while you can." Or possibly, "I bet *you* can't catch a fish this big."

Such a contrast.

I reach up to the nameplate of the painting. The letters of his name tingle my fingertips. It is a sensual moment, touching "Thomas Wiley," caressing "D'arcy," then blurring the two together. My mind is far away, in a world where Thomas, a nobleman, falls for me, a peasant who happens to be gorgeous in red. He is just starting to declare his love when. . .

"He was a total lush."

"What??!" I jump. How long has Darcy been standing behind me?

"The real Thomas was a hard drinker, womanizer—a total embarrassment to his family. He died in a pub fight in Sussex."

"Oh, gosh." In that unnerving moment, my daydream deflates and lies flat.

"I always liked this portrait of him, though. It is quite idealized, as though his parents wanted to show the world the man he never would be."

The fantasy is ruined. My hero, Thomas Wiley, is nothing but a cautionary tale. He is another freaking John Wickham.

I start planning another funeral for Thomas in my head. This time the eulogy has a decidedly different tone than the last one. "Today we say goodbye to Thomas Wiley—wimp, disappointment, and big brown squishy turd. . ."

I sigh. "I prefer the fantasy."

"I knew you would. Obviously, I do too." Darcy gestures toward the portrait. "I ignored the truth and borrowed a lot from this *illusion* when constructing *Pemberley*. Life and books will forever be intertwined. It is what we choose to see in both that determines the connection. Just wait. Thomas—the fantasy Thomas—has some great moments in my next book."

"Ugh. *The torture.* You're still going to make me wait, aren't you?"

The corner of his mouth turns up. "Yes."

I hate him for a split second, then love him all the more for his wish to offer me nothing less than perfection.

I find I agree with Darcy. I agree that we choose what we see. And I am grateful I chose to see Darcy for who he is. How easily I could have missed him.

Someday I would like to try my hand at writing too. I will write about Darcy, about this moment. About *us.*

Chapter 20

Back at Longbourn Library, Mrs. Phillips, proper and dainty as usual, steps up to the checkout with her stack of gardening books. Perennials, tulips, sunflowers, and lilies are the topics of the day, though growing season has ended. As I enter the books into the system, I pretend not to notice *Lady Chatterley's Lover* hiding among the group.

Mrs. Phillips's sunny smile matches the glory of the flowers; the glimmer in her eye conveys something else entirely. She slides the books into her designer canvas bag and carries them out.

After years of checking out books for Mrs. Phillips in the same combination—beautiful garden flowers with some "birds and bees" mixed in—I am starting to wonder something.

"Does Mrs. Phillips even have a garden?" I ask Mrs. Bennet in a low voice.

She puts her hand on my shoulder and whispers, "No, dear. She just *studies* gardening."

Ahh.

A dog bark sends my thoughts in another direction.

The dog, a St. Bernard, listens as a little girl reads to him from *Where the Wild Things Are* while she sits in the striped chair. The dog is all enthusiasm, looking about the room and licking at her face at random moments. The girl keeps reaching up to reposition his face toward the pages, taking her part of reading him the story very seriously.

It is "Read-to-a-Dog Day" here at Longbourn. The local animal shelter brought in a few of their most well-behaved canines to whom young patrons take turns reading a book. It is excellent reading practice for the kids and the animals thoroughly enjoy the attention. Often, the patrons walk out with a new pet at the end of the experience. It is a win-win situation, unless someone pees on the carpet.

A line of children hold their selected books, waiting for their chance to read to a dog. A miniature schnauzer puts his paws on a book and stares intently at the pages as a boy reads him *Clifford's Christmas.* It barks at what it imagines to be the most exciting parts.

Another boy pets a dachshund-poodle mutt that takes up his whole lap. The dog lays his head down and savors the story of *The Diary of a Wimpy Kid* as he drifts off to sleep.

A little Pomeranian trails a grouchy Mr. Bennet around the bookshelves. He gives me that "help me" look, but he is on his own this time.

Mary, terrified of dogs, stealthily creeps close to the wall, then tip-toes upstairs on some fabricated errand.

Darcy guides the next child in line toward the German Shepherd in Kitty's Korner. The girl, around six, clearly wishes she could read with any other dog. Tears start to form in the corner of her eyes. Darcy crouches down to her level and holds out a hand for the dog to sniff. The German Shepherd quickly assesses that Darcy is safe.

"Okay, hold out your hand," Darcy tells the girl. His voice is patient, sympathetic.

She slowly raises a hand, but cannot bring herself to uncurl her fingers that are clenched in a defensive fist. The dog sniffs a ring around the fist, then licks it.

The girl cringes and holds up the hand with the slobber toward her mom standing nearby.

Darcy laughs. "That just means he likes you," he says. The girl's mom nods in agreement.

Darcy gently coaxes her onto the carpet next to the dog. Side-by-side, the German Shepherd and his reader are about the same size. The girl's trepidation gradually transforms into a soulful reading of *The Poky Little Puppy*. The dog looks between the open book and the girl's face, taking in the moment in delighted bursts of energy.

I give Darcy a thumbs-up. He nods, then quietly steps away from the reading buddies.

Charlie has found his spirit animal in a Golden Retriever. He kneels next to it on the floor, helping a three-year-old girl read *Goodnight, Moon* to it. Occasionally, Charlie and the dog look up at Jane with the same bright expression on their faces. If it were not for the difference in species, they could be brothers.

"I have a feeling we are getting a dog," Jane tells me with a shrug of the shoulders. "Who could say no to that face?"

I am not sure if she is talking about the dog or Charlie.

Mrs. Bennet is now trailing the dog that is following Mr. Bennet. She tries to pick up the Pomeranian, but it jumps from her fingers, then wags its happy way toward Mr. Bennet once again.

Mrs. Bennet shrilly theorizes, "It's that bacon you had for breakfast, dear. You smell like bacon."

This event is going smoothly for once. The kids have not pulled any tails and the dogs are handling the change of venue well. They even left their marks on the library snowman outside as a Christmas gift.

And, of course, the volunteers are stellar. The tall one with the sideburns, particularly. Perhaps I am biased, though, concerning the guy I made out with ten minutes ago behind the bookshelf.

Georgiana flies to Hertford for Christmas and the Jane-Charlie wedding that will soon take place. In the process of dating her brother, I come to think of Georgiana as one of my best friends.

Georgiana and I are decorating a gingerbread house, and not very successfully. We sent Darcy out to get some more gumdrops and chocolate chips because too many ended up in our mouths instead of on the lopsided house. I add some icing to the gingerbread door, then squish a slice of licorice into it. I am making the whole thing worse, but at this point it does not matter.

"You know," Georgiana tells me as she makes a marshmallow snowman, "Will's like a different Will. For the longest time—years, really—he didn't laugh. He just *existed* after our parents died. I was the same way for a while, but it was like Will was just stuck in his sadness and his sense of responsibility to me. He poured all his energy into *Pemberley*."

Fitzy, sitting on a stool, sneaks a paw onto the counter. He pulls a chocolate chip toward himself and watches it fall then bounce on the floor. He tilts his head as though it is the most curious thing he has ever seen.

Georgiana lifts Fitzy off his stool and sets him on the floor where he plays with the chocolate chip.

I tell Georgiana, "I can see Darcy has loosened up a bit. You can't imagine what my first impression of him was." I accidentally break a mini candy cane and put it aside in the to-be-eaten pile.

"Oh, yes, I *can* imagine. I've seen him attempt to socialize with strangers my whole life. He's like a piece of dry toast. But I love to watch you interact with him. He actually *smiles* when you're around.

With you, he's looking forward to life."

"I need him too. More than you can know." I admit, "Honestly, I'd always hoped to meet someone in the library. Any real reader wants to meet the love of her life in a library or bookstore, I suppose. You can tell so much about a man by what he is reading. But I was foolish. I dismissed Darcy the moment I met him. I was blinded by nothing less than sheer prejudice. He's been very patient with me to overcome it."

"You two are lucky," Georgiana says. She places her elbows on the counter, searching for the right words. "You have a connection of minds most couples just don't have. You see each other's value. Well, it took you a bit longer to see his."

That is a truth, one that hurts every time I consider it. "I won't argue with that. I acted despicably."

"I remember when he told me he'd met a girl at the library. I could tell from the tone of his voice that she was special to him. He told me she was intelligent, humorous, beautiful. And she looked *right through* him. Apparently, you told him he was the last man you could ever go out with."

"Oh, don't repeat what I said back then." My stomach twists with the shame. I still cannot bear that I treated the man I love with such abhorrence.

"Don't worry—he doesn't blame you for those earlier slights. His biggest apprehension now is losing you."

Tires crunch the snow in the driveway, then the garage door makes a rumbling noise, indicating Darcy is home.

"Speak of the devil," says Georgiana. Then she gets up and heads toward the garage.

I walk into the living room and begin to peruse the magnificent bookshelf for the millionth time. Fitzy abandons the chocolate chip and trails behind me, always wanting to be part of the action.

Each book on Darcy's shelf has become a familiar friend to me over the past few months. There is a warm spot in my heart for the books I have already read, and an anxious excitement for those I have not. I marvel at the attentive organization of Darcy's bookshelf, how the books are separated into genres and alphabetized by author. I always know exactly where the books should be.

My fingers take a stroll through the fiction section, lightly touching the works of Alcott, Austen, Borges, Brontë, Chekov, Cervantes, Defoe, Doyle, Eco, Ellison, Faulkner, and, my personal favorite—Fitz. That is where my own sharp breath stops me.

The book I am touching is not *Pemberley*, but one titled *A Marriage at Pemberley*. By William Fitz.

The most intense book shiver hits me. It cannot be! Darcy said it would not be published for months! Why did he not *tell me*?!

I slide the book out. I attempt to open it, but I cannot. It is solid. It does not have, well, *pages*. What kind of evil trick is this? I flip the "book" over and over, anxious to solve the mystery. Finally, the discombobulation clears and I figure out the book is actually a *box* shaped like a book. I have seen such boxes. I work out which side of the cover is the lid and pop it open with my thumb.

Inside is another box. A tiny velvet one. I take a deep breath of anticipation. I set the book box down on the coffee table and open the velvet box just long enough to see the sparkle from the ring inside. The shock causes me to shut both boxes in a hurry.

A Marriage at Pemberley stays on the coffee table. Fitzy gives it a shove with his paw.

The living room becomes blurry. It is hard to move. I walk in a daze back to the kitchen. I sense Darcy enter the room and feel his kiss. Georgiana follows and starts unloading the groceries. I hear explanations of what kinds of gumdrops Darcy bought, but his words seem muffled and faraway. I mindlessly open a bag and start stuffing gumdrops into my mouth.

"Wait, Liz—are you all right?" Darcy asks. He gently touches my face and looks into my eyes.

It takes me a moment to find my voice. "Yeff," I say. It is hard to chew through all the sugary goo in my mouth.

"You look pale. Can I get you anything—a glass of water, perhaps?"

"Yeff." I keep chewing.

He rushes to the sink and fills up a glass. I gulp the whole thing, washing the gumdrops down.

Fitzy makes a long weird meow from the living room. Georgiana hears this, looks at my stunned face, and suddenly has an epiphany. She dashes off to the living room, where, undoubtedly, she sees the box sitting on the coffee table.

I stand up. I nod my head emphatically as I regain my composure.

Georgiana comes back to the kitchen with her hands behind her back.

"Liz is saying yes," she says. She is grinning now.

Darcy, quizzical and worried, says, "Yeah, I heard her."

I take a deep breath. "I'm saying *yes*."

Fitzy, now sitting in front of Darcy, meows impatiently.

"See, Will," says Georgiana, holding out the book box now.

"She's saying *yes*."

Darcy's confusion changes to comprehension. He accepts the box from Georgiana.

His face blanches now too as he turns to me. "I wondered when you would discover that. I have been anxious all day."

His hands start shaking. He opens the book box.

Georgiana stands back to watch. Fitzy looks between Darcy and me.

Darcy gets out the ring box and gently opens it. "It seems now is the time to ask you an important question, Ms. Liz." There is a bit of worry in his eyes. Is he still scared I will say no? *How* could I? *Why* would I?

Wait—he wore a *suit* to the supermarket to buy gumdrops? I will tease him about that later. For sure.

But right now I must erase all his doubt. "Yes, Darcy. You do not even need to ask. *Yes*." My heart is in my throat, my whole being filled with love for him.

Darcy laughs as his trembling fingers pull the ring from the box. "Just the same, I would like to proceed with the formality, if you don't mind."

"Just *ask* her already!" Georgiana insists.

Darcy nods. "As always, I bow to my sister's good opinion on matters such as these." He kneels down. His breathing is labored, but his tone is careful and lovely. "Ms. Liz. . ."

"It's Mrs."

He blinks a few times, then smiles. "Soon-to-be-Mrs. Liz, will you do me the honor of becoming my wife?"

"How many yeses mean "yes" to you?"

Darcy beams. "One more will do."

This time, I can barely say it, though. Tears of happiness are clouding my eyes and streaking my face. It comes out in a whisper: "Yes."

He places the ring on my finger and overwhelms me with his kisses. Then we hold each other until there is no doubt left.

Darcy is that book that I walked by dozens of times and did not think to open. Once I finally opened the "Book of Darcy," I could not put it down. The more I read, the more enthralled I am. You cannot pry it out of my hands.

The other men I dated were books I did not care to finish. Initially, they may have seemed interesting, but failed to deliver. I had no trouble putting them down and walking away.

Now I have a story in my grasp I hope will never end. William Darcy and me, forever. Best story I could imagine.

We marry in the spring.

Chapter 21

A young man walks into Longbourn Library with his borrowed copy of *The Hunger Games*, then hesitates to put it in the return box. There is a particular look on the boy's face: *captivated*. I often see that look of being transformed by what one has just read. I help him locate *Catching Fire*, the next installment in the series, and he reads ten pages before his mom forces him to check it out and take it home. I know he will be back in the next two days—he will *walk* to the library if he must—to get *Mockingjay* and finish out the series.

That is the enchantment books hold over us readers. When we see a room full of books, we do not see stacks of paper bound together. We sense magic.

I cannot believe it was only a year ago that I first set eyes on Darcy and his suit. Oh, how one year can change everything.

Charlotte and Collin still come for Tuesday Tea. Collin, who is managing Kate de Bourgh's new art-and-antiques shop, chats up everyone in the room. He prides himself on his "ability to mingle with those of any rank," whatever that means. At least he is not using his cringe-worthy pick-up lines anymore.

Charlotte's baby belly is starting to show. She has sewn maternity dresses for each stage of the pregnancy and is now starting on baby clothes and crocheted booties. I would love to throw her a baby shower in a few months, but I doubt she will need any gifts by then. I wonder what the baby will be like—short, myopic, plain, or all three? He/She will be well-tended and clean, without a doubt.

Through the gossip channels, we learn that John Wickham got shipped off to California once his stint in Reno was completed. A few law enforcement agencies there were anxious to discuss some of his actions. A paper trail, and another jilted ex who quickly identified him from a lineup, led to a further incarceration. John was guilty of check fraud and identity theft, as well as pretending to be human. So, now he practices his gratuitous swagger around a prison courtyard.

From what I hear of Lydia, she has moved on and has since been through two other boyfriends. I doubt John even crosses her mind now.

Kitty has thrived in the absence of Lydia's immature influence. Removed from Lydia's example, she has become more self-aware, less ignorant, and less insipid. Lately, all those hours of playing Lady Ambrosia to Denny's Prince Porkchop are starting to pay off. The extra time Kitty and Denny spend together outside of the puppet show is providing Longbourn Library with ample gossip. Mrs. Bennet's interference is a given. She is sure they are the greatest of the long line of couples she believes she has assisted toward married bliss.

Mr. Bennet remains the same.

Mary is finishing her last few days at Longbourn Library. She was accepted into a PhD program at a divinity school in Pennsylvania. As much as it pains me to admit it, she will be a difficult person to replace. She is a real one-of-a-kind.

Jane and Charlie Bingley—what can I say about them? The honeymoon ended, but they do not seem to realize it. They have settled into a three-bedroom house complete with and old cat, a golden retriever, and a large flowerbed full of daisies. Charlie started his own investment company and the locals are starting to entrust him with their harvest money. Jane and I often discuss our good fortune as we continue working at the library. With our husbands being such good friends, we look forward to raising our children alongside each other.

Georgiana, sister-in-law extraordinaire, is spending her semester doing a teaching internship in Taiwan. The time difference makes it difficult for us to chat real-time, but Darcy and I are thrilled to see Georgiana in different pictures: eating beef noodles with chopsticks; in front of Taipei 101 with eight shopping bags on her arms; standing at a whiteboard in front of enthusiastic Taiwanese children. It is exciting to see her living her dream.

Mrs. Hill and Mr. Fitz do not get along right now. They have not been on good terms since "Fitzy" ate Mrs. Hill's salmon. She growls and hisses at him as he sits innocently by, wondering what he possibly did wrong. But Darcy and I have a theory that it is all just a misunderstanding and eventually they will be best friends.

You would think I would be lonely with Darcy working at his desk all day, but my father is here now too. Darcy hired a private nurse and moved my father in once the honeymoon (Italy, *exquisite*) was over. My father loves to wheel himself around the house and flip through the zillion channels on the huge TV. His health has improved with the move. Something about having space and freedom has energized him. He brought with him a large box of books left over from my childhood. It is another hint of his hope for the pitter-patter of little feet about the place.

As for me, I am Mrs. Liz Darcy now.

Our married routine involves trips to the bookstore, Pablo Neruda poetry by candlelight, wet white shirts, and the sexiest heated discussions of literature. Occasionally, we go square dancing, but most nights we are content to stay in and enjoy a sitcom with my father. I still travel to work in my old truck that Darcy keeps threatening to replace.

I agreed to steer clear of Darcy's study where he is putting the finishing touches on his next novel. When he leaves the house, I find myself feeling like one of Bluebeard's wives, wondering if I should risk my husband's trust by venturing into forbidden rooms. So far, I have resisted, though. I only enter the study when he is there, steal a kiss or two, then leave him to his work.

Our biggest difficulty with married life so far is the same one all readers have after marriage: how do we combine our book collections? Between the book-themed bridal shower and the truckload of Amazon orders from our registry, we have plenty to deal with. Do we give up a duplicate copy when we have the same book, or do we hang on to the second copy because it has sentimental value and/or notes in it? And, where, oh, where are we going to build the other bookshelves?

Murial Rukeyser was correct when she said "The universe is made up of stories, not atoms." In my universe, an Idahoan and a Californian—a Goodwill sweater and a tailored suit—can fall deeply in love. I had never imagined it before Darcy, but is a scientific fact.

Epilogue

The lecture hall is crowded for William Fitz's first reading of his new book, *A Marriage at Pemberley*. I am sitting at the front next to where the author—a tall, alluring gentleman in a black suit—will be seated.

Jane and Charlie are sitting on the edge of their seats a few rows back. Their shared copy of the book is open with maybe 30 pages left to go. Jane turns the page with her thumb as Charlie reads over her shoulder. I wave and both look up, give me a happy wave in return, then go back to reading.

I sort through the other faces in the crowd. Collin is making his way around the room, shaking hands and repelling new acquaintances. Charlotte is at home with their infant son, Bourgh. Mary is absent, too, of course, but here in spirit. I see local professors, authors, cowboys, and "groupies"—oh, and now Kitty and Denny—a comforting mix of so many walks of life.

All readers. All fans of William Fitz.

Darcy stands at the front of the hall, talking to Mrs. Gardiner. He seems at ease, speaking with her amiably, with no hints of nervousness over this event dedicated to his talents and hard work.

Two women slide into the seats behind me. Their loud whispers are full of ecstatic expectation.

One says, "*That's* William Fitz. *Told you* he was worth the three-hour drive."

"Oh, *ding-dong.* Is he single?"

I turn around immediately.

"No." I look between the two women, one blonde, one brunette. "Most decidedly not."

The women's faces go from surprised to annoyed in an instant. I am sorry to ruin the fantasy for them, but that is my man they are talking about.

"I'm, well, *Mrs. Fitz*, so to speak."

The blonde woman raises an eyebrow and looks me over. It is clear she thinks I am lying.

I start to fidget. "See, I checked him out at the library," I say, then quickly realize how those words could be misunderstood at least two different ways. I shake my head. "Well, *he* was checking me out at first. . . Mostly, I just checked out *his books.* See, Longbourn Library hired me to do that. . . for. . .some. . .reason." I squirm. "And Darcy, or William Fitz if you prefer, read a *lot* of books and I kept checking him, I mean the *books*, out. To make a long story short, we got married."

Longbourn Library hired a bumbling idiot, going by the looks on the women's faces.

Ugh. I give up. I turn around and shrink into my chair, remembering why I tend to enjoy the company of books to the company of people most of the time.

And, here comes Mrs. Bennet for added emphasis. Mr. Bennet plods behind her, clutching two copies of *A Marriage at Pemberley.*

"Isn't this exciting, Mr. Darcy, eh, Mr. Fitz?" Mrs. Bennet's loud voice carries across four rows.

Darcy excuses himself from Mrs. Gardiner.

"Yes, Ma'am," he says as the Bennets close in on him.

"Welcome to the both of you."

"Now, Mr., eh, *Fitz*. Would you care to settle something between Mr. Bennet and me? As I read your book, I could not help notice that this character, Elizabeth, bore a striking resemblance to, well, *me*. In my younger days, of course, back when I was courted by *the handsomest* man in Hertford." She motions toward her husband. Her smile then turns to a disgruntled smirk. "*However*, Mr. Bennet disagrees with me. Said it was a fanciful notion if ever there was one."

Mr. Bennet shrugs his shoulders.

Darcy looks to me, amusement tugging at his mouth. He looks back to the hopeful face of Mrs. Bennet. "Ma'am, as you know I have been in Hertford long enough to hear the stories of your great love affair."

Mrs. Bennet gasps at the word "affair," perhaps thinking it a scandalous word. She rolls it around in her mind, trying it out for a moment, then smiles and nudges Mr. Bennet. "It *was* one of the great ones." She considers, "It still *is*, I must say."

Mr. Bennet slightly nods his agreement.

Darcy continues, "It is my opinion that these stories I've heard, of strong Idahoan women such as yourself, . . ."

Mrs. Bennet moves in closer, eyes wide.

". . .have greatly influenced the characters in my book."

"*Told you*, Mr. Bennet. *Told you*." She is well pleased. Smug through-and-through.

Mr. Bennet looks at Darcy and shakes his head. He will not hear the end of this for a long while yet.

Mrs. Bennet guides Mr. Bennet by the arm to their seats. She tells the man next to her, "Did you know that I was the inspiration for the heroine?" Everyone in the hall can hear that intrusive voice.

Darcy steps over and sits next to me.

I turn to him and whisper, "*Mrs. Bennet* was the inspiration for the character of *Elizabeth*, huh?"

"She might have been. It's all so blurry in retrospect."

"Conveniently blurry," I laugh. "There *is* another character I wonder about. He's a scoundrel, a rake, a real jerk—a guy curiously named John."

"I know the guy."

"Was he, perchance, inspired by anyone we know?"

"Sure was. But I don't want to give that one away."

"What are his initials at least?"

"His last name starts with Wickham."

"Gotcha."

I take Darcy's hand and he kisses my cheek. And, I secretly hope the girls behind us saw that act of affection.

I take another look about the room. The venue is now packed and a few unfortunate latecomers are stuck standing against the wall. This is Darcy's moment, the culmination of hundreds of hours sitting at a desk, putting word after word onto paper.

The early reviews say *A Marriage at Pemberley* is a masterpiece, a rare phenomenon where a sequel is actually better than the book before it.

I could not agree with the critics more.

Thomas Wiley does, as promised, have some great moments that show the strength of his character as he meets and falls for the seemingly out-of-reach Elizabeth Hale. She, this new heroine, matches his strength in every instance. The basic story is a classic one—a man and woman meet who do not seem to have a thing in common, but by the end of the book they are undoubtedly joined, undoubtedly equal. *Together.*

There are also some bits about knickers. Who would have thought?

My father wheels himself through the crowd toward his reserved spot next to me. He is awed by the number of people, the energy of the event. "All this for my son-in-law?"

"And his muse," says Darcy. "Don't forget about her, Dad."

"Proud of both. Very, *very* proud," says my father. He shakes Darcy's hand hard.

"Thank you, sir," replies Darcy. He sits up straighter, if that is possible. He is slowly accepting his own life of brilliance, one that cannot be compared to the illusions his ancestors created. I am privileged to be a part of it, witness to it—this moment, his life.

The audience is at last hushed.

The mayor stands to welcome the crowd and introduce the resident writer. Unlike Kate de Bourgh, Mrs. Gardiner seems to have read the book. Soon her "without further ado" has my husband on his feet.

Once the applause dies down, Darcy flips to a passage toward the middle of the book and begins, "Elizabeth said no more -- but her mind could not acquiesce. The possibility of meeting Thomas Wiley while viewing Pemberley instantly occurred. It would be dreadful! She blushed at the very idea; and thought it would be better to leave now than to run such a risk. . ."

Simply put, Darcy shines up there at the podium. All his unease is gone. His reading is smooth, confident—as unwavering as Pemberley itself.

"They were within twenty yards of each other, and so abrupt was Thomas's appearance, that it was impossible to avoid his sight. Their eyes instantly met, and the cheeks of both were overspread with the deepest blush. Thomas absolutely started, and for a moment seemed immovable from surprise; but shortly recovering himself, advanced forward, and spoke to Elizabeth."

Darcy pauses at the name *Elizabeth*, looks to me. He breathes in deeply, regards me with fondness and consideration.

We share a smile.

But Darcy continues his silent regard, the look in his eyes sliding from sincere to something more playful as the seconds tick on.

The pause goes on long enough that whispers erupt. Then a few giggles. My father nudges me and chuckles, donkey-like, to himself.

My heart does a few flips. I feel my face turning red as Darcy's dark eyes peer into that space we created when we let love in.

Sheesh, Darcy. If I were not already sitting down, I would have to.

"Keep going," I mouth.

He narrows his eyes, softly replies "okay" and continues reading where he left off.

My copy of *A Marriage at Pemberley* I pull from my bag. I had the honor of being the first to have one signed by the author. The fresh smell of "new book" hits me and the book shivers shoot through me. My fingers glide over the smooth pages, the glossy dust jacket.

There, next to William Fitz's signature, is the book's dedication:

For my dearest, loveliest Liz

Acknowledgments

Many thanks to Kyle Bascom, Tiffany Bascom, and Angela Kunz for their feedback and support.

I would also like to thank the Marshall Public Library in Pocatello, Idaho for putting up with my patronage.

Of course, I cannot forget to thank the incomparable Jane Austen, who was fond of writing, as well as reading, and who made the world a better place for it.

About the Author

Trudy Wallis is an ESL teacher and writer.

Made in the USA
Columbia, SC
28 December 2020